Breckenridge is Buried

Breckenridge is Buried

Henry Melton

Wire Rim Books
Hutto, Texas

WRB

Printing History
First Edition: January 2020
ISBN 978-1-935236-75-7

ePub ISBN 978-1-935236-76-4
Kindle ISBN 978-1-935236-77-1

Website of Henry Melton
www.HenryMelton.com

Cover Art by HMT STUDIOS Manila
Map data Copyright Google 2020

Printed in the United States of America

Wire Rim Books
www.wirerimbooks.com

Acknowledgements

When writing novels set on alien planets, I can't really visit and ask the locals for help, but Breckenridge is like a second home to me. I took a couple of visits to walk the streets and chat with a number of helpful people.

Special thanks to: Kurt Miller, Nick Pontis, Tara Olson, Richard Sims and a couple of hard-working guys who didn't want their names mentioned (you know who you are).

Roger Melton and Dr. Kevin Stephens were also helpful with details.

And I always want to thank my very helpful first readers and editors who do so much to correct most of my glaring errors; Jim Dunn, Linda Elliott, Mike Lynch, and Tom Stock.

Contents

Sunshine 1

Sunspots 7

What Just Happened 13

Research 19

What Did You Do 25

The Sun Burped 31

Power is Out 37

My Dad is Missing 43

In Trouble 49

Inventory 55

Not My Unit 61

Avalanche 67

You're Needed 73

Signs of Life 79

Not Even 85

Harris Street 91

Recharging 97

A New Start 103

Ski Hill Road 109

Hospital Run 115

Storyteller 121

Checking the Houses   127
Warmth   133
Rick's Problem   139
Relapse   145
Rick's Note   151
Misjudgment   157
Staying Alive   163
Nurse Kelly   169
House Rules   175
Exploring the House   181
Radios   187
Pillow Talk   193
Calling Anyone   199
Checking the Connections   205
Eve   211
Making Connections   217
Saying Goodbye   223
Packing Up   229
Epilogue   235
References   239

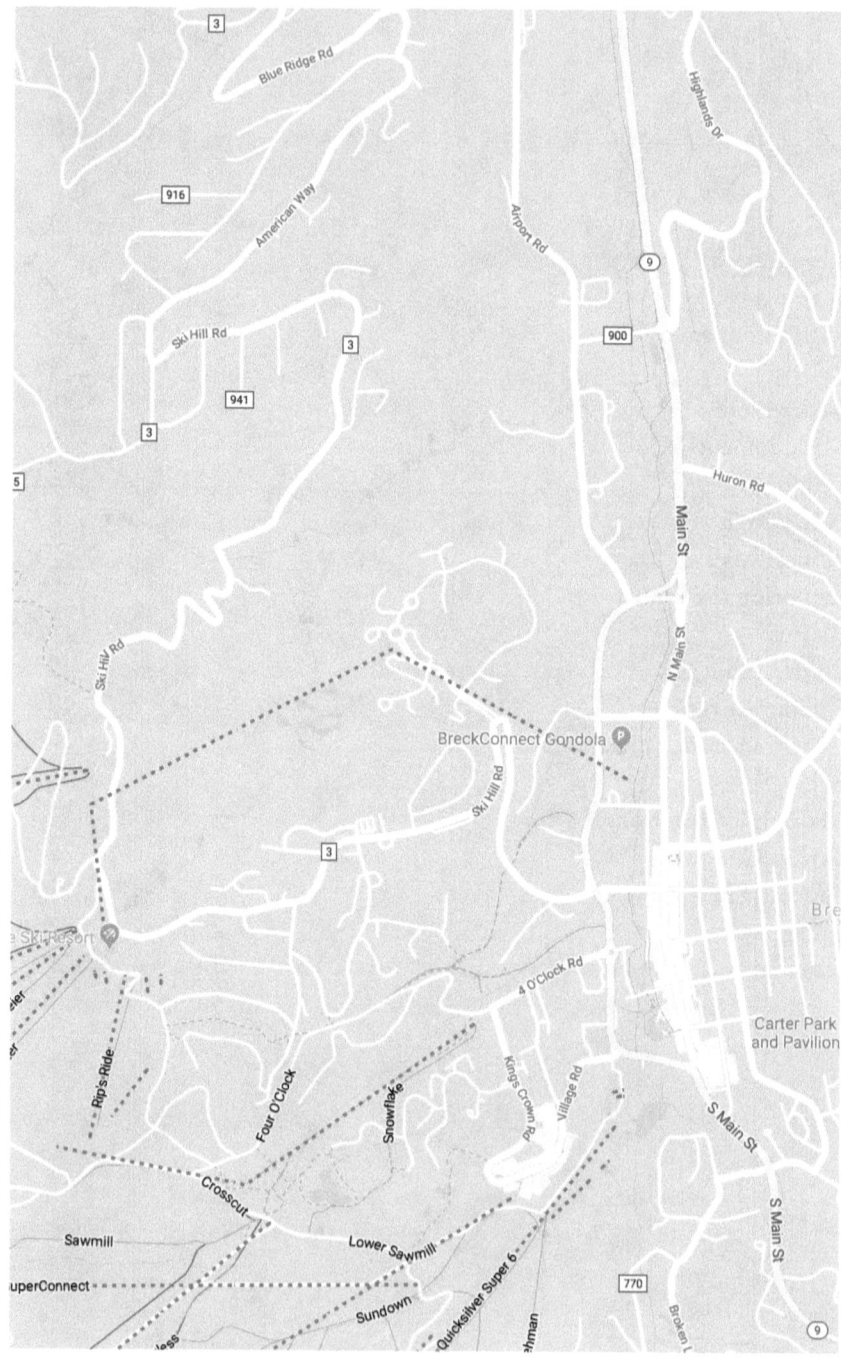

Sunshine

"Will, there's some sunshine," Ruth Dent at the front desk called out.

"Thanks!" Will Parker dropped the dust cloth and raced to the elevator, his glance out the window to the first floor deck confirming that there was indeed sun.

His father, Bob, managed the River Mountain Lodge, so he caught a lot of the grunt work when he was out of school. He really didn't mind dusting the lounge areas, but if there was sunlight, he had to act quickly. The elevator wasn't fast, but it was closer than the stairs, and all he had to do was get to the second floor deck as soon as possible.

As the elevator opened into the sitting room next to the windows the bright light of actual sunlight made him squint.

His telescope almost looked like a snow-covered Christmas tree hidden under its white dust cover. He'd chosen this spot for quick access just for times like these. He gripped the tripod through the fabric without even looking and lifted it, backing slowly through the glass doorway out into the snow.

He was wearing his jacket. It was, after all, Breckenridge Colorado in ski season, but he was wearing sneakers rather than his boots. He could already feel the cold seeping in as he shuffled through the snow.

Dad's going to want me to shovel all this off again. It's a lost cause.

He positioned the tripod right at the edge of the raised platform that contained the hot tub and put the legs at memorized positions. He pulled off the dust cover and aligned the equatorial mount. He'd done it so many times that the tripod was in position in just thirty seconds. Now, the scope with its battery-powered motors would track the sun's path through the sky.

He moved the scope by hand until the shadow of the telescope's long tube shrank to a perfect circle in the snow.

Safety check. He touched the sun filter just to make sure it was still there. It was a silvered Mylar cap over the front of the tube that blocked out almost all the sun's light—almost all.

He peered through the eyepiece and centered the sun's image. If that filter hadn't been in place it would have fried his eyeball. The sun was huge and bright, dotted with sunspots. Will fished his cellphone out of his pocket and placed it in the plastic cradle mounted in front of the eyepiece. A couple of taps after the phone autofocus made it sharp, and he captured three still images of the sunspots, and then switched to video and recorded thirty seconds.

At least he'd hoped for thirty seconds. The clouds moved in and blocked it out.

Will squinted up to sky. *No luck.* The break in the clouds was gone. Waiting longer in the cold was a lost cause. He retrieved his phone.

But he'd gotten his sunspots for the day. He rubbed his hands together and blew on them. Time to put everything back up. He looked for his dust cover, white on white and hard to see because it was already gathering more snow. He shook it off and fitted the cover over the scope.

He noticed, just a few feet away, one of the condo guests. A blonde girl about his age in a checkered sweater was watching his actions through her window. He nodded and smiled. He always smiled at pretty girls. Especially during ski season, there were a *lot* of pretty girls in Breckenridge.

He carried the scope back inside and made a stab at brushing off as much of the snow as possible.

"I was wondering what that thing was."

Will turned. *Checkered sweater, dark red slacks.* It was the same girl. "Hello. Yes, this is my telescope."

"What were you looking at?"

Will pulled out his phone and showed her. "I'm taking pictures of sunspots. I made a stupid mistake. This is my science fair project—observing the sun."

She looked at all the dots on the white circle. "Why is that a mistake?"

"I'm trying to measure how fast the sun rotates, so I need regular photos of the sunspots. All this in a year where we can barely see the sun. It's been snowing every day for a couple of weeks now, and it doesn't look like it's going to slow down any time soon."

She chuckled. "Yeah, I know. I'm Kelly. My dad is Sam Winslow. He got a bronze in the giant slalom in the last Olympics and he's up on the slopes every day practicing."

"I think I've seen you around. I'm Will Parker. My father is manager here. You'll see me shoveling snow and dusting the tables when I can't avoid it. Are you here long?"

She glanced out at the snow. "The whole season."

"Oh, are you going to one of the local schools?"

She hesitated. "Well … officially, I'm being home schooled, but Dad's not on top of things. When I get really bored, I'll open the books."

"I hope to see you around, then. But, I've got to get back to my chores before they notice I'm gone."

"Do you take pictures every day?"

He laughed. "That was the plan, one set of pictures every day at the same time, then measure how fast the sunspots move. But the way the weather is acting, I'm having to take shots when the sun peeks out, and that'll make the calculations a bit more complex."

"I heard you're never supposed to look at the sun, but I saw you looking."

"I've got a filter. It's safe."

"If the sun comes out tomorrow, show me, then."

"Okay. Room?"

"West 211."

"Nice talking to you. Gotta go."

. . .

"Will, are you done yet?" Bob Parker's managerial job was never-ending and he didn't hesitate to use his wife, May, and his son as extra hands.

Will glanced around. "Mostly."

"Well hurry it up and finish. We need to shovel the snow up on the second level. I've already done the front entrance and the first floor deck."

"Dad, I was up there a while ago, getting my sunspot pictures. Even with the sun peeking through the clouds, it was still coming down fast. I think it's a lost cause."

Bob sighed. "No help for it. People will be coming off the slopes and will need that hot tub. Make sure there are paths from both the east side and the west."

"Okay." Will wasn't enthused, but at least he didn't have to shovel the whole area, just passageways. That was a plus.

He finished off the dusting and bundled up. Dad was totally against using the gas-powered snow thrower on the decks because of the noise, so Will had to clear the paths with the shovel. The snow was knee deep already from the last time he'd shoveled it. The condo owners were all excited over the heavy snow. The more days the slopes were covered, the longer the units would be rented. It was a very seasonal business.

It didn't put any more money in his pocket, though. Dad gave him an allowance, but Will's work was tied to what needed to be done.

He started at the south edge, the only side where he could scoop the snow over the fence without dumping it on the deck below. On the first level deck, the east and west wings and the common corridor along the south formed a U-shape around the hot tub and the pool area. Will was grateful that the pool was already covered for the season, otherwise he'd have to keep the whole area shoveled, and likely several times a day. Up on the second level deck, it was smaller, but the snow seemed heavier there. He was the only guy at Summit High School who dreaded the weekend.

This is not the way he wanted to spend a Saturday. Probably Sunday would be a total loss as well.

He shoveled snow over the south fence, careful that it didn't pile up too high in any one spot, working back to the hot tub.

He was finished with the east pathway and working on the west side when the glass door opened.

"You've got to be kidding me!"

A big hairy black-haired guy in a swimsuit and his red-haired companion in a bikini stared at the expanse of snow blocking their way.

"Sorry!" Will said, "It's really coming down hard today." He shoveled as fast as he could, hoping to cut them a path through the last six feet.

"Well, duh! It's a ski resort! Or haven't you heard?"

The angry guy trudged through the snow with his bare legs and his girl followed in his footsteps. Will backed up to get out of their way. The man grumbled about idiot kids and the girl wouldn't meet his eyes.

Angry renters he could handle. Just smile, look humble, and stay out of their way. What he really hated was making one of the condo owners mad at him. The condo-owners association made the decisions, like whether to fire his father or not. The renters came and went, and while the reputation of the place was dependent on making everyone happy, sometimes you couldn't make a person happy even if you sweated blood.

The angry guy would likely be gone in a couple of days and he'd never see him again. It wasn't worth fretting over.

Trying to stay out of their line of sight, he finished up the shoveling job, dumped the last load of snow over the fence and hurried to get out of the cold. He glanced at W211's window, but the drapes were drawn. He hoped Kelly Winslow hadn't watched that encounter.

Sunspots

Will was working on his homework when his father stumbled in to the E105 unit where they lived. It was only eight in the evening, so likely Dad was just catching a nap. Will muted the music playing on his laptop and folded up his worksheet. He slipped out and found an empty table next to the big fireplace in the main lounge. His mother at the front desk gave him a look. He nodded. He could use the table as long as it wasn't needed by one of the other residents.

There were several other places where he could do his homework—the second floor lounge, the gym, and in the back of the office—but on a cold night like this, next to the big main fireplace was his first choice. *If I'm going to live in a resort, I should appreciate the amenities.*

He hurriedly worked down the list of math problems while he had the opportunity. His parents knew his homework was important, but when a guest needed something, that was *urgent*.

"Will Parker. Can I sit here?" Kelly, in her checkered sweater, smiled.

"Sure." He scooted his papers to the side and closed his laptop. "Just a getting the homework out of the way."

She curled her nose at the math worksheet. "Not my thing. I thought you might be working on your sunspot pictures."

"I can do that." He opened his photo collections. He selected a folder. The sun photos showed up in a slide-show format.

Kelly looked. "They're different colors."

He shrugged. "It depends on how bright the day was when I took it. The camera does color corrections automatically, and if the sky is blue, the sun looks a different color than like today when the sky was washed out with clouds. I don't really care about that. I might even make them all black and white when I make the video."

She tapped on the arrow keys. "What are you going to do with these sunspots again?"

He scooted his chair a little closer to her. He tapped the keys. "See how the dots jump in position as we flip between this picture taken today and this one taken three days ago?"

She nodded.

"If I have enough of these pictures, it's really easy to see the sun rotating. In my dreams I'd be able to take at least one picture every day and hope that some sunspots would last long enough so that I could see them make the second time around and count the days. As it is, I'll have to do it the hard way."

Will noticed his mother frowning at him. Bothering the guests was high on the list of things that could get him in trouble.

"What's the hard way?"

"A lot of careful measurements. I need to make a spherical grid that I can overlay over the sun's image so I can take each image and mark something like the latitude and longitude for the small sunspots and then I can take the timestamp on each photo and figure out how many degrees the spot moves across the sun in the three days and two hours, or whatever. I'll have to do that many times."

"Just the small ones?"

"I figure the small ones would be easier to locate precisely. The big ones change shape and I don't want to have to get into the problem of finding the exact center of an irregular shape. Look at this monster. It's been changing shape ever since it showed up."

He showed her several images back in time as it approached. "It should be dead center pretty soon."

"Why is it so big? Is it colder than the others?"

"I'm no expert. And it's not really all that cold. It's still thousands of degrees, it's just colder than the surrounding area."

He frowned. "Sorry. My mother is waving at me. Hang on."

He got up and went over to the front desk.

Mrs. Parker whispered, "Are you pestering the guests?"

"No, Mom. She came and sat by me. She's bored with her home school-ing and wanted to know about my science fair project. She's in W211, right near where I set up my telescope, and she saw me take pictures today."

She sighed. "I guess it's okay, but *don't* pester the girls. We can't afford to get that kind of reputation."

"I *know* Mom." He frowned. Like he'd ever had the chance to bother the pretty girls in their colorful ski outfits. *Thought* about it, yes. But he'd never taken the initiative.

Kelly grinned as he came back to the table. "Is your mother getting on your case?"

"Some. I'm not supposed to bother the guests."

"You're not bothering me."

He smiled. "Maybe it would be better to move somewhere else, out of Mom's line of sight. Hey, have you had supper? We could go over to Down-stairs at Eric's and have a pizza."

Kelly hesitated. "Not that I don't like the idea, but … well, you've got your mom and I've got my dad. He lets me take care of myself for the most part, but rule number one is that I can't date any ski bums."

Will laughed and put his hand to his chest. "Believe me, I'm not a ski bum. It's so rare I get to hit the slopes that it's almost not worth it having my lift pass. Between schoolwork and chores around this place, I don't have any spare time in the season."

She watched him with a slight smile. "I suppose I could call Dad and ask him."

She pulled out her phone and mumbled her request. Will tried not to listen in, but he could tell her father's voice had reservations.

Kelly put away her phone. "Dad's coming down."

Will asked, only half seriously, "Should I run?"

"No, nothing like that. He just wants to see what we're up to."

The elevator opened a couple of minutes later. The man looked younger than Will's father, but he supposed that was reasonable. Olympic athletes had to be in good shape.

As he pulled up a chair to the table, he held out his hand. "Hello, I'm Sam."

"I'm Will. Your daughter said you were preparing for the Olympics?"

He nodded. "A hard job, with all the new talent coming up hungry." He waved at the computer. "Kelly said you're watching sunspots?"

Will was struck by the pattern on the man's face. Goggles had left the skin around his eyes whiter than the rest of his face. It was obvious Mr. Winslow was out on the slopes hours on end.

"Yeah, it's my science fair project." He started on the same explanation he'd given Kelly, showing him the pictures he'd taken. Kelly added her two cents, explaining that the sunspots weren't really cold, just cooler than the surrounding area, so they looked black.

As Will explained the eleven-year sunspot cycle, due to peak soon, he wondered if the man was following all the details. He didn't want to judge, but there was no guarantee a full-time athlete was going to be that interested in the math and physics.

After a bit, the man nodded. "I never thought about doing something like that. Back when I was in high school, a baking soda volcano was best I could think of."

Will nodded. "I saw one of those last year. An old favorite."

Sam Winslow looked over at his daughter. "You can stay down here for a while. I'll wait supper for you."

He shook Will's hand again, and went back up the elevator.

Kelly said, "I guess that was a no."

"Sounds like it. Oh, well. I'll ask again some other time."

She sighed. "Pizza sounded good. I'm getting tired of frozen TV dinners. Neither of us are good cooks."

"Have you spent the season at Breckenridge before?"

"No. I've been at many ski resorts before. All over the world, actually. But I've never been ... settled in one place like this."

Will said, "I'll check the calendar then. There are a lot of special events, like the ice sculpture competition, that keeps the people coming back. I'll make sure you have a list."

She sighed. "I've heard there are good restaurants, but Dad has no interest in food. It's all fuel for him."

Will smiled, but had a sinking feeling. He'd love to take her out to the Hearthstone or some place like that, but the pizza at Downstairs would have likely broken his bank as it was.

Feeling like his opportunity was slipping away, he waved as Kelly went to the elevator to have TV dinners with her father.

He went back to his math worksheet. He still had to get that homework done.

What Just Happened

Will was up early Sunday morning to get the driveway into the underground garage scraped clear of the night's snowfall. There were always a few of the guests who visited churches in Frisco or Silverthorne.

His father pointed upstairs. "Go get the paths to the hot tub cleared out. We got a complaint yesterday. Shovel them four times a day if you have to."

Will didn't bother explaining. It wouldn't help.

He did the first floor level first and walked out onto the snow-covered deck. He could see the trails from yesterday, but fresh show had them softened into white channels. There was at least a new foot, whether from fresh snowfall or drifted in.

Surely the enthusiastic skiers were already taking the lifts to experience the trails where they could cut their own paths in the fresh snow. He'd better check the chemicals in the water while he was at it.

He stared up at the gray clouds and the snowflakes still coming down. No snow was a disaster to a ski resort, but at the other end of the scale was the Big Snow of 1898-9 where the town was cut off from the world. It was a local legend, and every heavy snow year was always compared to the Big Snow.

It'll never happen again. They didn't have snow plows back then to clear the roads.

Will sighed and hefted his shovel. There was no snowplow allowed at the driveway down into the parking garage level. On a Sunday morning, there was a good chance many of the people on the other sides of the windows would be sleeping in. It all had to be done by hand.

By the time he worked the second level deck, he cleared the west side trail first, just to make the angry guy of yesterday happy. The window to W211 had its drapes closed.

By the time he had cleared the routes to both second and first floor deck hot tubs, he noticed that the snow had stopped. He stared up at the clouds and nothing but gray stared back. There were no gaps to be seen.

But ... if the snow were letting up, even a little bit, then maybe it was a good time to clear off more of the snow. Sooner or later he'd have to clear the piles he'd made. Roofs were slanted for a reason. All this snow was heavy and he couldn't let it pile up without risking damage to the flat deck.

He spent another hour dumping snow off the north side of the building on the first level. There was quite a pile at ground level. If the sidewalk hadn't already been blocked by the snow buildup, he'd have worried about it. Dad would get out with the gas powered snow thrower and scrape it clear sooner or later.

...

The morning was busy. When he went back inside from shoveling snow, Mom sent him to the grocery store to pick up a list; mainly food for them, but also a few items for the main lounge. Hot chocolate and various coffee blends were popular with skiers. The alcoholic drinks were stocked by Jacob the bartender, so that wasn't his task.

But probably when I'm old enough to buy alcohol, they'll add them to my list.

He wondered from time to time what he'd be doing once he graduated. Colorado Mountain College was the only college he'd be able to afford, and with a campus just halfway down to Frisco on the bus route, closer than the high school, he would still be living at home. The sad thing was that the CMC campus in Breckenridge had great classes for someone who'd be running a restaurant or hotel, and almost nothing in the math and physics that interested him.

Riding the bus to City Market was a relaxing break. He often walked or rode his bicycle, but not on these icy streets. It was interesting to see which buildings had the soft pillow of snow on their roofs, and which showed the efforts of their owners to keep the build-up under control. The sidewalks were only partially cleared, but the snowplow drivers were putting in overtime keeping the roads open.

Now that the snow had stopped, for the moment, people were out and about. He hefted his carry bag. The aisles at the store would be crowded.

He was barely out, bag full, when he saw a dazzling patch of white on Peak 8. There was a gap in the clouds. Was the sun heading his way?

He had to wait ten minutes before the bus arrived, and it was clear, in just that amount of time, that he just might get some sunlight today—if he could get back home before the sun did. The sunlight dazzle crept down the slopes, heading for town.

He fidgeted in his seat as the bus made its way back. He was out of his seat in a flash as they stopped at the 4 O'Clock Run intersection and he dashed for the entrance to the lodge.

His mother was startled as he left her the bag and dashed for the elevator. "Sorry! I've got to catch the sun."

When the elevator opened up on the second floor, Kelly looked up with a start. "You're here. I saw the sun come out."

She had her hand on the cover of the telescope, as if she had been going to move it herself.

"Great. Hold the door for me."

He hefted the covered telescope and quickly walked it over to its spot. There was an inch of snow all over the paths he'd scraped clear earlier.

She watched as he quickly uncovered the scope.

"Don't look through the eyepiece until I've checked everything."

She nodded seriously.

The sun was out and he could feel its warmth on his skin. But it could all vanish in the next minute if the clouds decided not to cooperate.

Kelly watched intently as he moved the tube. "If the shadow is a perfect circle, then it's aimed at the sun. I don't dare use the finder scope and stare at the sun directly."

He felt the sun filter with his hand. "Always double-check the filter."

Then, he leaned over, peered through the eyepiece and used the adjustment knobs to center the image.

He gestured. "Take a peek. The little knob adjusts the focus."

Mentally, he urged her to be quick about it. The gap in the clouds was small, and their brief moment of sunlight was already half over.

She peered into the eyepiece. "Wow. That big sunspot is huge compared to the other ones."

She looked up, letting him move his cellphone into the cradle and take a couple of quick pictures.

She frowned. "It looks white in the middle."

"What?" He was changing the settings on his phone.

"The sunspot. It's got a bright white patch in the middle."

He hesitated and glanced through the eyepiece.

"That's impossible."

But what he was seeing couldn't be denied. In the center of the large sunspot, there was a bright white patch, more brilliant than the surface of the sun to the side of the sunspot.

Kelly asked, "What is it?"

Will mumbled, confused. "Some kind of solar flare? I dunno."

He switched to video and started recording, looking at the image on the screen. "That's really weird. I've never heard of a white sunspot."

Kelly said, "Does that mean it's *hotter* than the rest of the sun?"

"I guess."

But the wisps of cloud were drifting across the image. He looked up at the sky. The gap was moving elsewhere.

For a moment, he just stared at his phone, playing back the image. Kelly peered over his shoulder. He zoomed in to get a closer view, but it didn't make anything clearer.

He was aware that Kelly was expecting him to explain it.

He sighed. "I'm going to have to get on the internet and do some research."

"It's snowing."

He blinked, forcing his attention back to the here and now. There were a few snowflakes drifting down.

"This storm isn't going to give me a break! Come on, help me shake the cover. I need to get the telescope back inside."

Barely had they moved the telescope back inside than his father walked up.

"Will? What are you doing?"

"There was a moment of sun. I had to get my pictures."

Bob Parker glanced at Kelly, then outside at the path he'd shoveled through the snow. "The hot tub is clear enough for now. I need you to clear the sidewalks, especially around the back. The stores are complaining."

Will just nodded. His phone felt warm in his hand. He ached to get the pictures off the little device and on to the big screen of his laptop and just stare at them some more.

But Dad had spoken. He sighed. "Okay, is there gas in the snow thrower?"

"There should be enough, but check it."

Will gave Kelly an apologetic smile and headed toward the elevator.

He replayed the video on his phone as he went down to the parking level to get the little snow plow.

What had just happened on the sun?

Research

As if regretting giving him a glimpse of the sun, the clouds were dumping even more snow. Will walked the snow thrower slowly down the sidewalk between the rear parking lot and the narrow channel where the Blue River lay hidden under the ice and snow. He was grateful for the river. The snow had to go somewhere, and he'd rather shoot it over onto the river than on top of some guy's car or against someone's window.

It was a constant struggle. You couldn't just make the snow vanish, it had to go somewhere. He knew some people just dumped the excess into the street, waiting for the county to move it elsewhere, but Breckenridge was rapidly approaching the limits.

Front end loaders filled dump trucks with the snow and those piled the snow in nearby fields or built mounds in the parking lot, but Will wondered how long they could keep that up. It was snow season. The town needed those parking spaces to keep the skiers happy. Not everyone who skied here stayed in Breckenridge. Denver was relatively easy commuting distance, so he'd heard.

With the snow thrower, he had the sidewalks clear fairly quickly. He itched to get back to his computer, but he dashed up to the second floor to clear off the walkways one more time. The snow was coming down even harder than before.

That task done, he snatched up his laptop and went to sit in the storage room down on the parking garage level. The wireless connection wasn't very good there, but he was out of sight and his parents would have to hunt for him. He really needed some time to think and do a little research.

The first few searches came up empty. There were a ton of articles on sunspots, but as soon as he tried "white sun spot" or things like that, he got more product pages than anything. It was frustrating, fighting the unresponsive Internet and getting far too many junk results.

Maybe I can go back to my bedroom. At least the signal is better there.

He pulled the images back up and stared at the white spot. *That has to be a solar flare.* And when he zoomed out to take in the whole disk of the sun, he was struck by the symmetry of it all. *That is dead center.*

He knew that large sunspot had been moving toward the center of the solar disk over the past few days. It looked like it finally reached the center point.

If that's a huge solar flare, and it's aimed straight for Earth, what does that mean?

He changed his searches, hunting for "solar flare impact".

He didn't like what he found. Changing the search term to "solar storm" did the trick.

Wikipedia's entry on the "Solar Storm of 1859" got him to his feet.

He hurried up to the lobby.

"Dad!"

His father frowned and flicked his fingers, gesturing him into the back office.

"What do you need? And don't yell and disturb the guests like that."

"Dad, I think there's going to be a solar storm that will cause spikes on the power grid. I think we should turn off all the computers for a couple of days."

Mr. Parker frowned. "Will, we can't run this place without the computers. And don't we have protection—surge suppressors? And where did you get this idea anyway?"

"I saw a big solar flare when I was taking my pictures."

Bob Parker considered. "And when was that? Three hours ago? There's been no flickers. Will, I need you do concentrate on keeping the guests taken care of. Have you checked on the hot tub?"

"Yes, Dad. It's still coming down, but I had it cleared off an hour ago."

"Check it again. I don't need you to be borrowing trouble, getting excited over your science fair project. It's hard enough when you're off at school. We need to take advantage of the weekend to get these extra chores done."

Will sighed. He knew his father was deep in the process of ordering new supplies. The Christmas season was ramping up fast, and the early snows had caught him short-stocked.

Maybe I am just imagining this. How long does it take for a flare to reach Earth anyway?

He left his father and went up the elevator to check on the trails to the hot tub.

Kelly was sitting in the second story lounge, next to the telescope. She stood as he walked up.

"What did you find out?"

He shrugged. "I *think* what we saw was a Coronal Mass Ejection, a big bubble of plasma. It's the worst kind of solar flare, as far as I can tell. There was another one like it back in 1859. It caused auroras all over the world, down as far as Cuba.

"What worries me is that it caused the telegraph lines to spark."

Kelly frowned. "What's that mean for us?"

"I'm not sure. I could be borrowing trouble."

"Trouble like what? Radiation?"

"No. The Wikipedia article mentioned that back when, the telegraph operators had to disconnect the batteries that powered their lines." He sighed. "The thing is, we've got a zillion more lines than they had back then. Power lines, telephone lines—all that stuff. If lightning strikes a power line, it can knock it off line, and sometimes send a power surge. I'm going to make sure my laptop isn't plugged in to the charger. I told my father to disconnect the lodge's computers, but he wouldn't buy my argument."

Kelly frowned. "I have a desktop computer. Maybe I should unplug it."

Will nodded. "I certainly would. The thing is, the flare we saw was three hours ago, and there's no surges yet. I need to go do some more research."

"How long does your battery last?"

He shook his head. "It's old. No more than two or three hours. I need to narrow this down. If it's even a real thing to worry about."

She said, "I saw it, too. You have pictures of it. Are you sure this is the same thing as what happened in 1859?"

He nodded. "A couple of scientists were observing the sunspots back then. They even have sketches of what they saw. Bright white spots in the middle of a large sunspot."

"Sounds familiar." She shifted from one foot to the other. "I'm going to go unplug. You do your research and call me when you get more information."

He nodded. "After I shovel some more snow, but I'll do that quickly."

She sighed in exasperation. "Can I do that for you? You need to find out more about this solar flare. We might not have time."

Will shook his head. "A guest shoveling snow for me? My father would never forgive me if I let that happen. I'm fast. You just take care of your computer. And what's your number?" He handed her his cell phone and she entered it.

He broke records getting the trails cleared to the second floor hot tub, and then raced down the stairs to the storage room where he'd left his laptop.

The Wikipedia page was a gold mine, with a big list of related links after the article. As he discovered new information, he texted Kelly.

Will: It's called a Carrington Event, named after one of the amateur scientists who reported it.

Kelly: Amateur? Like you?

Will: Like us. You saw it first. But we'd only be scientists if we report our sighting.

Kelly: Do that.

Will: Later. In 1859, there was a delay of 17.6 hours between the white flare and the Earth effects — auroras and such. Fastest on record. Most CME's take more than a day to arrive.

Kelly: So ... Sometime in the morning?

Will: More or less.

Kelly: I'm going to get my cellphone and booster battery charged up before then.

Will: Same here.

When Daylight Savings Time went away the week before, sunset abruptly came much earlier, now before 5 PM. It was even worse in the valley which ran north-south where the mountains blocked the horizon. Official sunrise and sunset were something of a joke, only good for seeing when there would be sunlight on the peaks.

And that's only true when the clouds cooperate. If the CME arrives on schedule, it'll be early morning.

Early morning on a Monday. The chances are he could be riding the bus to school when it hit. *If I'm lucky, I might get to skip school.*

His opinion shifted a little later when he downloaded a report written by Lloyds, the insurance people. They had tried to estimate the damage that would be caused by a Carrington Event. It was disturbing. Maybe if he were lucky, nothing would happen.

Will: If we get a big one, electricity might go out for a Long Time.

Kelly: How long?

Will: Weeks, months, years. It depends on how many transformers get fried. They only have so many spares. I'm worried.

Kelly: I tried to tell my dad, but he doesn't believe in this stuff. I tried to get him to take a break from practice tomorrow, but he's got an early lift up the mountain with one of the food crews.

Will: Did you warn him the power might go out?

Kelly: Yes, but he doesn't believe me.

Will: Same with my folks. The thing is, I'm not sure myself. What if morning comes and it's an ordinary day? I'll feel stupid.

Kelly: But relieved.

Will: Exactly.

What Did You Do

Reading first hand reports from the nineteenth century, details from the Quebec 1989 power grid failure, and a report of a 1972 CME that arrived even faster than the 1859 Carrington event all spilled over into his dreams when he finally went to sleep.

He woke with a start. He looked around, but there was nothing but the glowing digits of his alarm clock. It was five. He'd gotten maybe three hours of sleep, but he shook off a dream where he went to school and found out that everyone else already knew all about solar storms and they'd been having them regularly every year and he was the only one who didn't know about them.

He closed his eyes, but he didn't feel at all sleepy. If his CME was as fast as that one in 1972, then it had already arrived. Maybe it was all over and he'd missed it. The '72 one hadn't knocked out the power grid. Little CMEs happened every few decades.

Regardless, with all these clouds, I'll never get to see the auroras.

The most spectacular auroras of a lifetime might be going on overhead and he would never get a chance to see them.

I'll never see anything here in my bed.

He got up and dressed for the day. Quietly, he crept out the unit and down the hallway.

"You're up early," said Greg Turner, the night manager.

Will nodded. "Yeah, I couldn't sleep. Have there been any problems?"

Greg chuckled. "You sound like your father. No. It's been a quiet night."

"I'm going to check on the snow on the second floor deck."

Greg shrugged. He looked back at the papers he was working on.

Barely had the elevator door closed than he tensed. *Stupid. I shouldn't be riding in the elevator when I'm expecting a power outage!*

But he made the one-floor ascent with no problem. He tried to remember what the emergency procedures were in case of someone trapped in the elevator. *I'm sticking to the stairs for now.*

He stepped out into the snow, five inches deeper than when he'd left it last time. He stared up at the sky.

The moon is up. Even though it was overcast, he could tell that much. The thinner patches of the cloud cap weren't quite as dark, but even the thicker clouds were tinged orange with the reflection of the street lights. With the clouds so close to the ground he wondered if the sky was clear up on the peaks. He was tempted, but it was be stupid to try to ride a lift now.

Off to the north, he could see the gondola, but it wasn't running. He doubted any of the lifts were running this early, but he could see headlights on the slopes. Snowmobiles and snow cats were active, getting the people to work at the dining places that dotted the slopes.

Kelly said her father was getting an early ride up the mountain, probably hitching a ride with the workers. He looked over at her window. It was dark. Maybe Mr. Winslow was used to getting up quietly as well.

After a few steps through the snow, he sighed and went to get the snow shovel. He wanted to be outside for as long as possible this morning, and he'd be better to be exercising if he wanted to keep from freezing.

...

Thirty minutes into the scrape and heave rhythm, he'd cleared the path to the hot tub, but he kept at it, dumping snow off the side, just so he could have more time with the waking town. When he went around the fence and walked through piles of snow where he could see over the Blue River, there was more of the town to see. Lights came on as people woke up and shop owners arrived to get ready for the day.

Dawn brightened the clouds and he could no longer see the orange glow from the streetlights. He expected them to go out before too long. People were out walking on the sidewalks. One guy looked in a hurry.

He's going for donuts, I bet. If he had enough spending money, he'd invite Kelly to the Columbine for omelets.

Then, the streetlights flashed brighter.

"What?" He paused, staring over the town. Other people stopped in their tracks as well. One lamp flared even brighter and went out.

It's happening!

But if it was burning out the streetlights, what was it doing to the lodge?

He looked up high, but if there were aurora, then the clouds and the morning dawn kept them obscured.

He dropped the shovel and ran for the doorway.

In the hallway, one of the lightbulbs popped in a flash. Will raced down the long zig-zag hallway racing for the stairwell.

"Excuse me!" He swerved around a startled lady in the hallway and hurried down the stairs two at a time.

He came out on the parking level and hurried to the circuit breakers. He reached for the main cut off switch. He barely grabbed it and pulled when lighting arched out and knocked him across the floor.

...

"Will! What did you do!" Bob Parker came running up. "Did you turn off the power?"

"Dad! Don't!" He reached out to stop his father, but sparks arcing across the contacts did that for him.

"What in the world!"

"Dad, I told you. Solar storm. Keep clear of it."

His father reached down to help Will up. "Are you okay?"

"Teeth rattled. My arms are still tingling."

His father frowned at the circuit breakers. "Is it over?"

"No! Stay clear. It could last for hours, or more."

"Will, tell me what's happening." The man listened carefully as Will spelled out what he knew about solar storms and what they might do to the power grid.

Together they used a few mops and buckets to put up a warning barricade around the breakers in case one of the staff or even one of the guests decided to investigate.

Will explained the basics to his parents and Greg Turner once they got back to the office.

"The sun blew a big bubble of electrified plasma our way. Bigger than the Earth. All the wires on the telephone poles picked up a charge and are frying equipment, light bulbs and anything else that might be sensitive. The phones are probably out as well."

Greg picked up the telephone. "You're right. It's making cracking noises, but no dial tone."

"Put that down. It could zap you."

Greg dropped it back on the cradle.

His mother nodded toward the front desk, where there were three people. "What do we tell them?"

Will said, "Tell them it's a major power outage. We don't know how long before power comes back up. I guess we should warn then to stay clear of electrical equipment and phones as well."

Greg said, "I can't get any signal on my cell phone either. No bars."

Will nodded. "I was out on the deck when it happened. Streetlights flared and burned out. Probably the cell towers are out as well."

Bob nodded. "I'll go tell them. Greg. Make up a sign we can post to let people know what's going on."

The two men parted to their tasks.

Will's mind was racing. "Mom. There's going to be a run on the grocery store as *everyone* tries to stock up. And the credit card machines won't work."

She nodded. "Cash only. I guess I'd better go get at the head of the line." She picked up her coat from the rack behind her.

"Will, how bad is this?"

He shrugged. "Pretty bad. Every time I think about it, I can see things are worse than I thought they were before."

She nodded. "Our stove is electric. We might need to get the grills out of storage."

He hadn't thought of that. He sighed. "I need to make a list."

His father came back into the office just as his mother left. "Will, the automatic parking garage door won't open. Some of the guests are trying to leave and they can't. You'll need to help Greg and me get it opened manually."

Will nodded. *At least I don't have to worry about catching the school bus.* It was going to be a busy day.

By the time the guests had packed their cars, which was a trial since the elevator wouldn't let them bring down all their luggage on a trolly, there were five other families who were preparing to leave early.

Bob nodded. "I'm glad to see them go. Power failure or not, we're responsible for taking care of the guests. The fewer mouths to feed and fewer rooms to keep warm, the better for the rest of us."

Everyone was bundled up. The lodge had residual heat, but most rooms were heated with baseboard electric heaters. Even the many gas-log fireplaces were often controlled by electric switches and igniters. It was going to get colder.

They disconnected the garage door from the motorized chain and lifted it manually. Will stood guard, keeping the entrance cleared during the hour that seven cars drove out. He was nearly ready to pull the door back in place to keep the snow from drifting in, when one of the cars returned.

"Is there a problem?" Will leaned down to the driver as he opened the window.

The father of a family of four looked worried. "Can we change our mind? Check back in? All the gas stations are closed, and I don't have enough gas to make it home."

Will waved. "Go ahead and park. Talk it over at the front desk."

He was sure his father would make arrangements for them, but he'd been trained. It wasn't his place to make decisions like that. Send them to the manager.

The Sun Burped

Mrs. Parker returned from her grocery shopping, laden down with twice the bags she usually had. She didn't look happy.

"I almost didn't get anything. There was already a crowd and the clerks were trying to work around the power outage. There were candles lit and lanterns at the ends of each isle. Only one checker was taking credit cards, and she was backed up. They had the old-fashioned credit card receipts and the slide machine to get the imprint. Some of the people were angry that their credit cards no longer had the embossed numbers.

"I got through okay, but only because I knew Kathy Simms, one of the clerks, and had cash to pay. I concentrated on staples—flour, cornmeal, and some ground meat. I figured volume more than flavor, for now."

She shook her head. "Kathy said they had to keep the store open. They were afraid the place would be looted if they tried to close. Better to have employees there keeping an eye on everything."

Will helped her move the supplies to the pantry, all of them that would fit.

"Mom, I'm going to go check with the city to see if they've got any news on how long this will last."

She nodded. "Don't stay too long. We'll be needing you more than ever during this disaster."

...

Town Hall was just across the street, but there was a big hand-lettered sign in the window, "CLOSED DUE TO POWER OUTAGE. CONTACT POLICE FOR ASSISTANCE." There was a city map taped below it with the sheriff and the police locations circled. The sheriff's office was just on the other side of the grocery store. Will didn't wait for a bus. It was less than a mile, a fifteen minute walk—maybe more in the snow.

As he approached the sheriff's office, he saw a man on the roof with a broom, sweeping the snow off the south-facing solar panels.

How many places have solar panels? Those will be valuable if the power grid is down long. It ought to make some electricity, even with the clouds.

There were a dozen people clustered around the reporting desk. A couple of battery-powered lanterns had the place lit.

The deputy said, "No. There won't be any news until a car gets back from Frisco. Radio and telephone are out. You'll just have to wait. Write your emergencies on the clipboard and we'll get back to you just as soon as we can."

A gray-haired man with a curled up mustache mumbled to the man next to him, "Maybe it's a nuclear attack. I've heard that if the Russians attack they could set off a high-altitude H-bomb and wipe out all communications."

Will spoke. "No. It's a solar storm, the biggest one since 1859. It disrupted the telegraph lines back then. If it was a nuclear EMP, then everything would be fried, not just things directly connected to the power grid. Solar flare CME's work differently."

The man looked his way, but turned back to his conversation. They weren't going to listen to him.

Will pushed his way up the line to add his entry on the clipboard. It was already folded over several sheets. Hand-lettered at the top was Name and Complaint.

Will wrote down his name and gave the situation at River Mountain Lodge; no power, no heat, and not enough food to feed the guests that were stranded.

He added, *"One guest tried to leave, but the gas stations are all closed. The police need to protect the gas stations and grocery stores against looting. See if there is a portable generator to run the gas pumps.*

"I know exactly what happened. There was a solar storm that electrified all the power lines and fried the power grid. It isn't just local. It's world wide. We have to prepare for the long haul. I have documentation on my laptop for as long as the battery lasts."

He handed the clipboard back to the officer.

Will asked, "Why is the radio out?"

The man shook his head. "The car units and the handhelds work, but the main communication center was burned out. Cars can talk between themselves, but we can't reach other towns and I can't run dispatch to the mobile units."

Will nodded. Only the radios that were plugged in were fried. He waited in the crowd for a little longer, listening. There had already been two auto accidents with intersections where the lights weren't working. Deputies had been sent to set up temporary all-way stop signs all along Highway 9.

The officer said, "The traffic lights won't be back quickly. They were fried. Controllers, too. They're still sparking. It's not just a matter of turning the power back on and replacing the bulbs."

Will gave up and headed back. Across the street, in the same shopping center as Central Market was a gas station. He walked in.

"We're getting ready to close."

Will nodded. The convenience store aisles were emptied of food and drinks. "Do you have a generator to run the pumps?"

The clerk shook his head. "I wish. I could probably charge ten bucks a gallon, if I could only run the pumps. You should have seen it earlier. Tourists were swarming the place like it was the end of the world. I had a cop helping me keep order. Have you heard anything? People are saying the power grid was shut down by hackers."

Will shook his head. "Nope. Solar storm. It's the same all over the world."

"A what?"

Will gave him the short version.

The clerk, probably only five years older than he was, shook his head. "So people knew this was coming? Why didn't they warn us?"

"They only knew it would happen eventually, not when. And when the sun flared, that only gave us a few hours warning. I saw it happen, but who's going to listen to a high school kid?"

...

As soon as he reported back to the lodge, he was sent to visit all the rooms to warn everyone that there would be no electric heating and get them to pull their drapes to conserve heat.

"Well then, fix it!" The same guy who had yelled at him about the path to the hot tub was still at the lodge, unfortunately. "I've got a fireplace, but it doesn't work either." The man flipped the fireplace switch on and off repeatedly.

"It's an electric valve." Will said, not sure that he was getting through to the man. "I'll talk to maintenance."

He moved on to the next room before the man could demand he do something else impossible.

For the next few hours, he was constantly on the move. He still had to shovel snow—that wasn't slowing down any. But he also had to drain the hot tubs. With no way to keep them heated, Dad wanted as much of the water gone as possible before it froze solid and burst the pipes.

Ruth Dent and the maids who usually commuted in from nearby towns where housing was cheaper never showed.

...

People gathered in the main lobby, and Will moved as many chairs as possible into the area. With the big wood-burning fireplace as the main heat for the area, the place was overrun with smaller children as families moved as the air in their rooms got chilly.

Some of the warm air was making its way down the hallways, so people close to the lobby were propping their doors open, just so that they could get some of that heat.

Above the main entrance there was a open space, with balconies all the way up to the fourth floor. Will had been sent up to each of the upper floors to partially open the doorways to the balcony area so that warm air could seep into the other hallways.

Bob put his hand on Will's shoulder. "Spread the word. We're having stew at five. We'll have a meeting at the same time. I want you to explain what this solar storm is and what it means."

...

Even though he rehearsed what he was going to say, facing the crowd of people didn't make his nervousness go away, especially with the constant clatter of silverware on the ceramic bowls, and a crying baby.

Where is Kelly? I haven't seen her all day.

"I'm Bob Parker, the manager of River Mountain Lodge." His father's voice caused the noise to drop a bit.

"This power disaster has thrown us all for a loop. Vacations are over and we're all just trying to stay warm and fed, with a roof over our heads. To be honest, I didn't sign up to run a soup kitchen." There were a few chuckles.

"Our old arrangement is canceled. I'm not keeping track of how many days you're staying. After this is all over and you're all safe at home, this mess will be some accountant's nightmare. But for now, we're partners. We have to pull together.

"The electric heaters are all out. The same with your stoves. I have had many questions about the gas log fireplaces in the units. Unfortunately, even if we could bypass the electric valves, the gas pressure is dropping rapidly.

"So please, please don't try to use the plainly marked gas fireplaces in the units. They aren't designed for wood fires, and we just can't afford a fire that would put us all out in the snow.

"There are only dozen units out of the eighty with wood fireplaces. I'm asking that as much as possible, that these places keep their door opened to share that warmth. There is a pile of firewood on the south end that we can all share.

"This fireplace will be running constantly, even if we have to chop down all the trees around the property. We've moved the portable grills next to the gym so we can cook without venting the smoke into the living areas. We've got a couple of cooks, but if any of you have those skills, you help would be appreciated.

"Please unload your refrigerators and build up our food supplies. It's not going to help anyone to hoard spoiled milk. The grocery stores are emptied out, not only here but in Frisco, Dillon, and Silverthorne."

A voice called out, "What caused this? When will we get power back?"

Bob turned to Will. "Do you want to answer that?"

Will stood up. People looked at him.

"The sun burped." There was an uneasy laugh.

Will nodded. "It does this all the time. The fancy name is Coronal Mass Ejection, or CME for short. The thing is, the bullet has to be aimed in the right direction for us to even notice. Scientists have seen these before, but most of them missed us.

"In 1989, a smaller bullet knocked out the power grid in Quebec and caused a cascading power failure on the East Coast. In 2012, there was one this size, but it missed us.

"When the CME hits, it builds up a huge spike in all the wires strung across the countryside. It's like a lightning strike hitting the whole world at the same time. It fries the transformers on the power lines and zaps the phone circuits. The last time one this big hit, back in 1859, the only wires we had to worry about were telegraph lines, but they sparked and they had to disconnect the batteries. The effects were observed all over the world."

An unfamiliar voice asked, "How do you know all this?"

Will looked in that direction, but it was dark everywhere but near the fire.

"Pure luck. I've been taking pictures of sunspots for my science fair project. I saw the flare happen, and when I hit the Internet trying to figure out what I saw, the only thing that matched was the 1859 solar storm. I was up all night researching this stuff, just hoping that I had it wrong."

His father interrupted. "I'm glad you came by, Sheriff Thompson. Could you come up here where people can see you and answer some questions for us?"

Power is Out

The man in uniform looked as uncomfortable as Will felt. He frowned at the people. "I can tell you one thing. Staying off the road is a wise move. I've been handling accidents all day. It's better now that we've set up stop signs, but the weather isn't helping. With the radio dispatch down, it's hard to coordinate with the snow plows."

He looked at Bob. "You're better organized here than most of the hotels and condos. Quite a lot of the population, resident and tourist, are sitting on their hands and waiting for the lights to come back on. Let me tell all of you, what the boy said matches what we've heard from people who've made it this far from West I-70 and from the trickle that came over Loveland Pass.

"Power is out everywhere. Even if the electric crews can bring it back up easily, Breckenridge is a small town off the main roads. We're not high on their priority list. We'll have to take care of ourselves for awhile.

"The county is coordinating with the city and organizing crews to cut firewood. Any able-bodied men who can help keep their families warm need to show up at the main parking lots. Believe me, it's a lot better than sitting in your car with the heater on, risking carbon monoxide poisoning until your gas runs out." He sighed. "Let me tell you about the idiots I've seen out there."

A man raised his hand. "Is it any better in Dillon?"

Thompson frowned and shook his head. "I didn't want to bring up all the bad news at your meeting here, but I-70 is closed. The bad weather was forcing all the tanker trucks and hazardous material traffic that couldn't handle Loveland Pass to build up a convoy that could be escorted through the tunnel. When the power went out—something happened and several tanker trucks were hit by a car that went out of control. It caused a big spill at the east end of Eisenhower Tunnel. With the power down, we can't get the clean-up crews in place and the fumes are so bad than an engine spark would trigger a bad explosion. Both eastbound and westbound are contaminated. And now with the power out, the ventilation system that normally keeps the exhaust fumes cleared out is down.

"All the traffic from Denver is stopped. We tried to send them back on the eastbound lanes, but they came right back. There's another blockage somewhere near Georgetown. I fear I-70 is blocked all the way back to Denver. Refugees that could make in over Loveland Pass are struggling to find shelter in Keystone and Dillon.

"All the traffic from the west, trying to get to Denver, is caught here as well. Dillon, Frisco, and Silverthorne are all overloaded with refugees. There are some people risking north to Kremmling or south to Leadville, but you'd better have full gas tanks before you start, and that's no guarantee that the highways will be open. If more radios are down, it'll be that much harder to keep the snowplows running. I don't recommend it."

After a few more questions, Thompson whispered to Will, "We need to talk."

Will nodded, but he was more than a little worried. He had known the CME was coming and he hadn't warned the police. Was he in trouble for that?

The meeting dissolved into smaller discussions. Some families took their children back to their rooms while others bundled them up in blankets in range of the fireplace. Will led the sheriff back to their unit.

"I read the comment you left on the clipboard," Thompson said. "You claimed you had documentation on this situation?"

Will pointed to his laptop. "I can show you, but the battery is old and I can't guarantee it'll stay on long. I wish I could print it out, but...."

Thompson nodded. "No power for the printer."

Will booted up the laptop, frowning at the power indicator. "Let me show you the most important stuff first. This is the analysis Lloyds did on what the storm would do to the power grid."

Will stepped him through the documents, pointing out the most important parts.

Thompson frowned. "Two trillion dollars in damages?"

"That's what they say, and they're the insurance experts, right?"

"Can I get a copy of these documents?"

Will rummaged and found a flash drive. He winced a little as he deleted some game software, but this was more important. Watching both the copy progress and the battery bars, he sighed when all the PDF files were transferred.

"I'm sorry I didn't try to warn you ahead of time, but I only had a few hours to try to decide if this was real or not. I wasn't really sure until the light poles started sparking."

Thompson shrugged. "Oh, we had a warning. But until you explained it a few minutes ago, I had no idea what a CME was. The message the station received over the statewide alert system was less than useful. It didn't explain what was going to happen, or when, or what we should do about it. And if you'd come knocking at the door, we wouldn't have paid you any more attention than that alert. It's all so unbelievable."

Will was a little relieved that someone else had noticed the sunspot and had acted on it.

But just then, the laptop went black. He sighed. "Sorry, the batteries are just ancient in that thing. I can't bring it back up without plugging it in."

"Then, just tell me what you read."

Will pulled the flash drive and handed it to Thompson. "Hopefully you'll have a computer that can read these, but for practical purposes, the history stuff is fascinating, but can't help us now. The damage is done. The real question is how long will it take to get the highways cleared and the electricity back. Just looking at this place, we can't even guess how many things burned out until the power comes back on."

Thompson nodded. "That's what they tell me at the station, too."

Will asked, "I was wondering, those tanker trucks that were lost at the tunnel—were those meant for us?"

"Possibly. In any case, I don't expect fuel deliveries for a while. Food either."

Will played with ideas he'd been considering. "We've got gas stations that just need a portable generator. Probably we could wire around the credit card stuff. Most of the cars in the parking lots could be siphoned as well, if you could get permission."

The policeman nodded. "We're already handing out IOUs for the things we need to requisition. Right now, food and firewood are the highest priorities. We might be calling on you to join a work crew, but your father probably needs your help the most."

Will frowned. "I really wish the snow would take a break. I'm wearing out my snow shovel. Now is not the time to challenge the Big Snow Year record!"

Thompson shuddered. "Don't even say that. We've got to get supplies shipped in as soon as possible or we'll have people starving or frozen in their houses." He shook his head. "Don't tell anyone I said that."

...

Will walked with the sheriff to his car and watched as he drove off. With a long sigh, he hefted the snow shovel and tried to clear the main entrance again. Halfway through the task, he watched as the big yellow snowplow rumbled through, clearing southbound Park Avenue.

As long as the snowplows keep the main roads clear, it won't be too bad. Those burn diesel, don't they? Surely they've got extra tanks of that, right?

It was surprising how dark it was outside. There were no street lights, barely any traffic, and all the buildings looked deserted, whether they were or not. All sensible people were huddled around a fireplace somewhere.

He set the shovel aside and walked out onto the crunchy ice and stared up at the black overcast sky. *No dancing glow. If there's any aurora left, then it's not strong enough to get through the clouds. Maybe a little glow that way. The moon?*

In the middle of the intersection, he could see a few fireplaces glowing red in the distance on the east side of town where old houses were. He wondered if single family homes would be better off? Maybe if they had full pantries. Some of those places were built before everyone relied on electricity.

It was quiet, too. No nightlife. No couples out walking the shops on Main Street. No music playing.

How many people had gone to bed early, cuddled up in as many blankets as they could manage? It had been a very long day for him and his family. His own bed, suitably padded with more blankets, called to him.

But he listened, and if he closed his eyes and stretched his senses, there was still life in this town; a faint murmur of conversation off in the distance, some vehicle's engine running several blocks away.

And, was that the shush of skis on snow? Was someone really out here in the dark, skiing?

He listened carefully. There was a rhythm to it. Not a downhill skier, someone was putting their weight on one foot, and then on the other. Cross-country.

Will nodded. If he were better at that, Nordic skiing made sense for getting around.

Then he saw motion in the darkness. Someone was heading south on Park. He'd better move out of the way.

He moved carefully back to the side of the road, back to the main entrance. But the figure turned and came his way.

In the faint light shed by the moon behind the clouds, he could see details as she came closer.

"Kelly! Is that you?"

In the dim red light from the fireplace that reflected out the main entrance door, he could see her pull the muffler from her face. She looked panicked.

"Will! Is there a policeman here? Sheriff Thompson? The deputy said I could find him here."

He put out his hand to steady her. "What's the problem? Thompson left several minutes ago. He drove off south, and I don't know where he was headed."

She sagged. "Will, Dad is missing! He never came off the mountain."

My Dad is Missing

"He was up on the mountain. I talked to one of the cooks who works at The Overlook. As they were evacuating, he saw Dad hiking up the hill toward the Back 9 trail. They didn't think anything about it since Dad was an expert skier and there's not any slope he can't handle.

"But since then, no one has seen him. Everyone scattered their own way and no one kept a tally of who was on the slope. I talked to the police and they said to check with the sheriff.

"Will, I'm afraid Dad is caught up there somewhere and no one is looking for him. If I can't find Thompson, I'll just have to go up there myself and hunt for him."

"It's dark, and how are you going to get up there in the first place?"

"I can climb a slope. I've done it before."

Will shook his head. "My family has a snowmobile. I'll take you. I'll need to get a heavier coat."

She nodded. "I've got to change my flashlight batteries, too."

"I'll meet you in the lobby. Have you had anything to eat?"

She blinked. "No. I haven't had time."

"You have to have something or I can't take you up the slope. It's too dangerous."

She nodded and unfastened her skis. He went on ahead inside.

A quick look around and he couldn't see either of his parents. He hurried over to their unit and he entered quietly. As he suspected, they were both sound asleep, gently stirring mounds under a pile of blankets.

I can't wake them now. Both of them have been hard at work all day. And they might just refuse to let me take the snowmobile.

He found the keys to the self-storage unit and bundled up. It was going to be cold up on the mountain.

Kelly was waiting for him, chewing on a protein bar.

"Is that going to be enough?" he asked.

She patted her pockets. "I've got more."

He said, "We've got to go to our self-storage place, first right off the highway, north past the traffic circle."

She nodded, "Go ahead. I'll beat you there anyway."

He nodded, jogging through the ice and snow at a slow-paced slog. It was the best he could manage. Not long after the first parking lot, she passed him, gliding on her skis a lot faster than he could manage.

I've really got to learn how to do that. Is there any place still open that would sell Nordic skis?

Not that he had any money for that.

He was hot and sweaty under his coat by the time he saw her waiting at the self-storage building.

"This one," he called. He found their unit and had to warm up the lock before he could turn the key.

She turned on her flashlight, just enough for him to check the gas and top it up from the five-gallon jug they'd left there from last time. It had only been a month since Dad had checked it out, so the gas was probably still good. In his memory it had been a warm sunny day. Would those come back any time soon? It seemed like this snow was going to last forever.

He dug out the snowmobile suits. "Here, put Mom's suit over your coat. You'll need the extra warmth." He put his on as well. They fumbled in the dark, with the limited light of the flashlight.

The one-piece outfits made it hard to move, but he had experience. They needed more than just jackets on a night like this.

The engine started and he realized he'd been holding his breath. They moved out of the shed with a couple of jerky lurches. Kelly's skis were strapped beside her standing tall above her head.

"Can you drive this thing?" she asked.

"I could last spring. Give me a minute to get used to it."

She held on. He could barely feel her arms around his chest through all the padding.

"Save your flashlight." He turned the headlights on.

He knew he wasn't supposed to drive the snowmobile on city roads, but this was an emergency, right?

Nervousness about driving right past the sheriff's office building took him racing down Main Street and then turning at French Street. From there he could drive up the Gondola Ski Back trail and head up the 4 O'Clock Run.

She slapped on his side and he slowed down.

"Yes?"

"I've got my radio. I need to stop to call for him."

He could see the blue plastic in her hand. Many people used family radios like that to keep in touch on the slopes. He wasn't surprised she had one.

"Daddy! Can you hear me? I'm looking for you. Please reply!"

She held the speaker to her ear, then shook her head.

"Do you have a special channel?"

She nodded. "We always use seventeen. Dad got the more powerful ones when the FCC rules changed."

"Okay. Hang on. Signal me when you want to stop."

They powered up the slope. Will tried to stick to the most traveled part of the path, where the snow had been packed down hard. He'd had to dig the snowmobile out of soft drifts before and it was no fun. It occurred to him that they were up here on the mountain by themselves with no backup. Probably he should have alerted the police that they were doing this.

Stupid. I'm not used to this kind of stuff. Real rescue people have procedures to follow.

But it was too late to turn back now. Kelly had a few paths she wanted to follow. They paused again and she made her radio call. There was no answer.

Breckenridge ski slopes were spread out over several mountains in the chain, from Peak 10 to Peak 6. It was huge and he'd never skied all of it. If the story Kelly was given was true, Mr. Winslow was on Peak 9 and it was unlikely that he'd hike to the other peaks, especially if there was an emergency situation going on.

Still, if they were on the same peak, surely they'd be in range of her radio, right?

"Kelly? Is your father's radio okay? Fresh batteries and all that?"

She was behind him, so he couldn't read her face.

Softly, she said, "I hope. I have to check frequently. He could be buried."

Will felt stupid. *Right. There might have been an avalanche. What else could keep an expert skier from coming off the mountain. If he was buried under snow, then his radio signal would be weak.*

From 4 O' Clock Run, they took Crosscut to Sawmill and followed the Peak 8 SuperConnect lift.

"Dad likes to slalom around the towers when he gets the chance."

Will got the idea that Kelly would often be right there with her father, when they had the chance to ski together.

"Kelly, you'll have to guide me past this point. We're getting into all black territory and I don't have these slopes memorized."

"Okay. Stop at the branch there."

He waited for her to make her call.

She called a second time.

"Did you hear something?"

"I don't know. It could have been static. Go up another hundred feet."

He frowned. The snow was getting a lot harder to maneuver in. The slope was steep and it was all fresh powder. No one had skied this way all day and the night before. The snowmobile was getting bogged down. He hoped Kelly didn't want him to drive all the way up to the top of some double-black.

"Dad? Is that you? I'm here, on the slopes, looking for you."

Will heard the reply. It was weak. "Down. Buried. Waving my pole."

Kelly frantically waved her flashlight around. "I can't see you!"

Will asked, "Which side of the slope?"

"Dad? Which side of the slope are you on?"

There was static. The signal was weak.

"Say again? I can't hear you."

"Right! My right."

She got her hand under control and scanned the slope on their left. The snow looked pristine.

Will said, "I'm going to move up another few yards." He revved the engine and lurched up the slope. Something caught his eye and he stopped.

"There! There's a fallen branch." The weight of the snow had broken a limb on one of the large pines.

Kelly scanned the snow around it. She yelled. "I can see it!" She keyed the radio. "Dad, I can see the tip of your pole. We're coming."

Will gunned the engine and put them just downhill from the glint of metal, waving just a couple of inches above the fresh snowfall.

Getting out was like swimming. The snow wouldn't hold their weight. They had to dig their way toward him.

And he was down several feet deep. He was coughing when they finally dig down to him. He gasped for air when Kelly brushed the snow off his face.

"Collapsed my breathing hole." He coughed again. "I've got a broken leg."

Will nodded. "Okay. We'll be careful."

In Trouble

"I'm really glad I saved battery life for your call." Sam Winslow held his daughter's hand, glove to glove. "When that branch took me down and I realized my leg was broken, all I could do was call out on my radio. But nobody answered."

Will carefully eased the man's broken leg into the snowmobile suit he'd just shed. It was cold, but Winslow needed the protection more than he did. The snow had formed a protective blanket over him, and as long as he kept his breathing hole cleared, he had a place to wait for rescue.

As soon as he had the man suited up, Kelly and Will together could drag him across the snow and fit him into the rear position.

"A real rescue team would have a sled, sorry."

Winslow coughed, and said, "It's real enough for me." He coughed again.

Will didn't like the sound of it. Did he have pneumonia?

"Kelly, let's go straight to the sheriff's office off Park Lane. They'll know which hospital to take him."

She nodded. "If I get there before you do, I'll let them know you're coming."

It sounded like a brag, but he suspected she was just being honest. She could ski.

"Okay, but go exactly the same route we came up. It's not a night to be out skiing on your own."

She laughed. "Hear that, Dad? But yes, I was counting on your headlights."

Turning the snowmobile around so it was heading down the slope took several trials and some shoveling by hand to dig the runners out of the snow, but Kelly didn't take off until he was moving.

The wind chill cut right through his coat, and his teeth were chattering as they made the run down to town.

On the final turn on Gondola Ski Back, there were car headlights aimed up at them. Kelly took off like a rocket and zipped on ahead.

Will wasn't surprised when the police car's flashing lights came on. Who else would be out driving at night?

He pulled up beside Sheriff Thompson.

The man shook his head. "I saw the lights on the mountain. I didn't realize you were that crazy."

"Sam Winslow has a broken leg, and maybe hypothermia. We need to get him to a hospital."

With Thompson's help, they were able to ease him into the back seat of the police car.

Kelly said, "I'm going with him. Can I take my skis?"

Thompson had straps and fixed them to his car.

He asked Will. "Will you be okay?"

"Yes. I've got to get the snowmobile back into the shed. But I'm fine. Go on."

He watched the car pull away and felt the weariness descend on him. He was tempted to go park the snowmobile behind the lodge, but his father would frown at that. Now was not the time to get the snowmobile stolen.

He took the deserted streets back to the storage shed and backed the snowmobile back into its slot.

Oh, Kelly and her dad have the suits. I hope I can get them back.

With the locks secured, he trudged his way home. The exercise helped keep him a little warmer, but he was chilled to the bone by the time he got back to the unit.

I need a hot shower. He unfastened his coat. *Oh, yeah. No hot water.*

He used his flashlight to pile on blankets and crawled into bed. He curled up and shivered. It wasn't long before the fatigue had its way.

. . .

His mother called. "Will, time to get up."

Later, he heard her again, off in the distance. "Will? You can't sleep all day. There's work to be done. Get up."

Then, still later, there was a shake on his pile of blankets. His father's voice said, "Will? I need to talk to you. Get up."

Will clawed his way out to the cold air in his room. He blinked up at his father's face. The rough hand felt his forehead. "You don't have a fever do you?"

"No, I'm okay." He blinked the sleep from his eyes. "What time is it?"

"Morning. Late. If you've got your old Timex, then dig it out. Alarm clocks aren't working any more."

"Okay, I crashed. I was up late."

His father nodded, not smiling.

"Sheriff Thompson came by and asked about you. What's this I hear about you being up on the mountain in a snowmobile? Was it ours?"

Will sat up on the side of the bed with his blankets wrapped around his shoulders. "Yes, I had to."

"You didn't ask, and you know you don't have permission to use the snowmobile without permission. And in the middle of the night?"

"Dad, one of our guests was missing! Sam Winslow. His daughter Kelly was frantic and was going to climb up the trails by herself looking for him if I hadn't insisted on helping."

"And you didn't even ask, just snuck the keys out and left?"

"I was going to ask. But you and Mom both were dead asleep. After yesterday, I couldn't wake you up and ask you about this."

"Yes, you should have done that. Will, I understand this was a rescue, but you and this girl could have gotten yourselves in big trouble out there on the slopes. You know how easy it is to get bogged down in heavy snow."

"Dad, I know! I *did* have to dig myself out a couple of times, but then, Winslow was buried four or five feet deep in the snow and he'd been stranded out there all day long. He'd have died if we hadn't found him when we did. If we'd have waited to put together a bigger rescue party, the pole he was using to keep a breathing hole open would have been totally covered by the new snow.

"We'd never have seen him. As it was, we only found him because Kelly knew his habits and they had walkie-talkies. Even then, we had to be almost right on top of him before she could hear his radio, as buried as he was."

Bob listened with a frown. "You topped up the gas before you started?"

"Yes, the jug we left in the shed was only a month old. I knew it was good. I made her wear Mom's snowmobile suit, and it was a good thing we had them, too, because he was really chilled.

"Dad, both suits are still with the Winslows. I didn't have a chance to recover them."

His father sighed. "Well, I guess that can't be helped."

Will said, "I'm not sure where they took him, but Kelly went along with her father."

"Thompson took them to the St. Anthony Summit Hospital."

Will nodded. "Good. He looked in bad shape."

His father sighed. "I can't like it that you went off on this rescue without letting me know, but he was one of ours. We have to take care of our guests. But just because you're getting away with this one time doesn't give you permission to use the snowmobile without asking."

Then he frowned and looked at the window. "But get up and grab your shovel. The weather's gotten worse."

Will frowned, "Worse?"

"Yes, we need to get the snow off the roof, and it's too dangerous to do it alone."

...

The heavy swirl of snow filled the air. It hid the peaks and most of the town as they worked. Mr. Parker had climbing gear they used as safety lines as they shoveled the snow, sending it off the four-story drop to the ground below.

It was a long task, complicated by the structure of the lodge, with well over a dozen roofs, connected into the east and west branches of the building. The place was built on a slope as well. The front was a floor taller than the rear. Too much of the snow was dumped back into the center deck where Will would have to scrape it off again.

But it was a necessary task. Snow could build up heavy enough to collapse roofs in bad seasons, and this was one of the worse.

Will paused to catch his breath, perched on the peak. It looked like the snow was easing off. He could see the peaks vaguely in the distance and more of the town could be seen. The whole place looked wrapped in a white blanket.

Off across town, someone was honking a horn. He tried to locate it, but most cars were just pillows on the blanket. Another few days of snows like this and some would be hard to see at all.

He squinted. There were some people out on the street.

"Dad!" he yelled.

"What?"

"There's a fire! There's a house on fire."

Inventory

By the time Will and his father climbed down from the roof and hiked the four blocks through the snow, the old, wood-frame house was plainly done for. Flames were flaring out the windows and the roof was collapsing. There were thirty or more people gathered around, but their main concern was keeping the fire from spreading to the neighboring houses.

With no pressure in the pipelines, people were scooping up buckets of snow and fighting the flames as best they could. There was no sign of the fire trucks.

Will shoveled snow into buckets, in the vain hope that the flames would melt them. Other helpers snatched them up as soon as he filled them. He realized that some of the people were firemen, by the Red, White & Blue Fire District shirts. They had to walk in to help.

A police car showed up far too late to do anything but add a couple of more hands to the bucket brigade. They couldn't even get the vehicle closer than a couple of blocks away. Will didn't recognize the policemen. Sheriff Thompson was probably off doing something else.

The rumors were that the fireplace had gotten out of hand, and that certainly matched what Will saw.

The house to the north had blisters in its paint, but quick work by the bucket brigade had saved it. The trees between the fire and the house to the south had saved that house, but the trees were charred.

Nobody was seriously injured, but the town had five new homeless. Before Will thought to ask his father if there was room at the lodge for more people, neighbors had taken them in.

More people were arriving as the news spread farther, but there were more hands than needed. Some just came to gawk.

Mr. Parker gestured. It was time for them to go. There were plenty of people available to keep an eye on the remnants of the house.

Will followed his father back to the lodge. He went straight into the cooking area.

His mother looked up. "Was it a fire? People are talking."

Solemnly, his father nodded. "One of the old houses on French Street. Burned to the ground. A fire that got out of hand." He looked at the grills that had been brought indoors. "We need to get a better handle on this."

She nodded. "We're down to one tank. If we don't run out of food first, we're going to have to find a way to cook over wood."

"We can't make any mistakes, or we'll burn the lodge down. Maybe we can make an outdoor stove."

She winced. "I can just imagine cooking in this weather."

"We may have no choice."

"Then find us some more food. We're running short already."

...

Bob Parker made announcements while everyone was collected around the fireplace, eating dumplings in chicken broth. Will listened as his father gave a firsthand report of the house fire and repeated his warning not to try to use the gas-powered condo unit fireplaces.

He also said, "Starting tomorrow, we'll be coming around to inventory the owners' closets for items that can be useful, like heavy coats, extra blankets and any stored food items. I really hate to use people's things without permission, but we're in a special situation.

"In addition, there's a problem with the locks. Although we replaced the batteries in the card-key locks recently and normally they should last eight months or more, the batteries weaken in cold weather. If you leave your room and find out that you're locked out, come check with us. We have a way to work around it. But, if you lose or damage your key, we have no way to make you a new one. The house computer system is down for the duration.

"You could also prop the doors open. It's not likely a burglar could get through this crowd."

There was some laughter. Most people were stuck at the lodge all the time, so the deserted hallways of last week were gone. There was always someone in sight.

Will felt the master key in his pocket. Dad had warned him.

His father's instructions had been simple. "Get up early so you can use the daylight. Just write down the inventory for now. We'll have to replace everything we use once the power comes back up."

Will walked down the hallway, and then on a whim, went up to the second floor. He knocked at unit West 211, but there was no response. Kelly was likely still at the hospital with her father.

He unlocked the door with the master key and went inside, using his flashlight sparingly to look around. There was no sign that she'd returned. There was the clutter she'd left when she was still hunting for her father.

He didn't have the owner's key, so it wasn't the time to do the inventory for this room, but he just had to be sure that she hadn't come back. He was always busy. He could have missed her.

This power blackout was really an adventure, if he could just get his mind around that. Just because he was working long hours didn't mean it wasn't something rare and unusual that he should savor.

It would have been more of an adventure if Kelly was around. He hardly spoke to anyone but Dad.

. . .

Will woke at the first hint of light and rummaged for his old watch. He'd been putting it off for days.

Wow. It's still got battery.

But the time was obviously hours off. No way was it eleven fifteen.

He dressed and stumbled out into the dark hallway. There were a couple of men also dressed for work outdoors.

"Morning, science-fair guy."

Will didn't remember their names either. "Morning. Are you heading out?"

The taller one nodded. "We're just trying to remember the words to the Lumberjack song. Do you remember it?"

"Sorry. It never crossed my radar." He looked at the man's watch. "Um, do you have the time? My ancient Timex is confused."

The man smiled at his watch. "It's a Rolex GMT-Master II. If it's a second off, I'll eat it. 5:03 AM and twenty seconds."

Will hurriedly set his watch to match, as well as he was able. "Thanks. I haven't used a watch in a couple of years and I really need it now."

The shorter guy held up his arm, showing a pale band of skin on his arm. "Yeah. I love my Apple Watch, but I've got it stowed away until I can charge it again."

"Are you guys going to cut firewood?"

"Yep. Second day at it."

The short guy nodded. "I've got muscles aching that I didn't even know I had."

Will nodded. "It's a bad year to be on snow shoveling duty, too."

The three of them walked to the makeshift kitchen. Will introduced himself. The taller one was Owen Turner. The smaller was Greg Kirk.

The cook on duty was Christine Kirk, Greg's wife. The lumberjacks had lunch pails to take with them. Greg sneaked a peek. "Smells good at least."

His wife swatted him on the arm. "Just be lucky you've got something nutritious. Supplies are running low."

Will scored a potato-sized dumpling for breakfast and shoveled the night's snow for a while. He decided to hold off knocking on people's doors until at least 8 AM. He was hardly going to be welcomed as it was—digging into people's closets.

Almost all of the condo units were independently owned. The owners often stayed at their own units just a week or so out of the year and left it up to the management company to rent the places out to the tourists the rest of the time. Typically, there was a locked closet in each unit where the owners kept their skis, coats and other personal possessions stored away while the renters were there.

Will had to inventory all those things, in case there was something they could use during this crisis. He didn't look forward to the task. It was like digging into someone's underwear drawer without permission.

But it was his task. Maybe his reluctance was keeping him out in the snow a bit longer than he planned.

He looked up at the noise.

Off in the distance, a siren was approaching from the south.

Hurriedly, he tramped over through the snow to peer over the wall. Trailing a cloud of snow, a police car moving far too fast for the ice-covered road zipped down Park Avenue.

He listened as the siren faded in the distance. At least the trouble wasn't close.

People were coming out of buildings all over town. A siren wasn't something to be ignored. After that house fire, a lot of people realized that disasters required everyone to pitch in. The police and the fire department just weren't up to the task of handling it alone anymore.

Will could hear conversations even from down the street. With the lack of traffic noise and without the normal bustle of the tourists, the town stayed quiet.

Nobody knew what was happening. Will shook his head. He would find out eventually. But for now, he had a job to do, and he couldn't put it off too long.

Not My Unit

Will knocked on the door. After a moment, the door opened a crack. A woman's voice asked, "Yes, who is it?"

"This is Will Parker, the manager's son. I'm here for to inventory the owner's closet."

"Oh! Yes, I remember. Um. Could you wait a bit?"

Will nodded. "No problem." He held up his clipboard and made a note. "Do you have a better time? And don't bother to clean the place up. It makes no difference to me. All I'm interested in is any supplies that the owners left in their closet."

"Okay, just give me thirty minutes. Sorry."

"No problem." He looked at his watch and noted the new time. "I'll see you then."

He moved on to the next door down the hallway. Luckily, this one was empty. He knocked anyway, and then used his master key after there was no response.

He opened the drapes to let in some light and could immediately tell that the room hadn't seen any cleanup since the previous persons checked out. It wasn't a horrible mess, but chairs were askew around the kitchen table and there was trash on the counter top. He found the owner's closet quickly enough and used his flashlight to rummage through the contents. He noted down the coats and ski boots, the little artificial Christmas tree and too many other items to make a complete list. Still, he had enough information in case they quickly needed another coat or something.

The whole process took about fifteen minutes. He locked everything back up and went on to the next room.

This time, a wide-eyed six-year-old boy named Jason was at his elbow the whole time, asking questions about what he was doing, what notes he was taking, and what each item in the owner's closet was. Will had to hunt for the labels to figure out what the rice cooker and the other cooking tools were. All of them were electric, so although he noted them down, they were sure to be useless for his purposes.

Jason was absolutely fascinated by the master key that would open any room and the box of keys, each with a tag that told which room each owner's closet key would unlock. Will was sure such a key to massive treasure stores would haunt the little boy's dreams.

He promised to see Jason again sometime and then, when he was done, went back to the first unit. The woman had obviously spent the whole time sweeping and cleaning. For a unit with the water turned off, and no electricity, she'd done a Herculean task getting the place polished up in such a short time. He wondered if she always kept her unit clean.

In contrast, the owner's closet was piled to the ceiling with smelly shoes, numerous kids toys, coats, boots, blankets, spare pillows and sealed cardboard boxes that he just didn't have the heart to unpack and inventory. He only hoped that the lady couldn't see all the mess that he could. He knew it would nag at her clean streak.

He took his notes and locked everything back up. It was time to move on the next unit.

...

By noon, he'd visited over a dozen of the rooms and collected pages of notes. There were high points. A couple of the rooms had, in addition to an owner's closet, an owner's pantry. Both of them had dry staples like bins of rice and flour, numerous spices, and canned goods. He was sure his mother would have him raiding those rooms immediately, leaving a detailed IOU to be paid after things got back to normal.

One room had a thirteen-year-old girl named Cassie waiting for him—hallway gossip had let her know he was coming. She had fixed her hair and dressed in her fanciest coat. She stayed close and a couple of times bumped up against him as he worked.

She made a point of letting him know that her father was off helping the city and that her mother was down on cooking duty. She asked if he had a girlfriend.

Will had little experience in being the object of attention for a girl, but she was a bit too young for him, and he still had hopes that he'd see Kelly again, not that he told Cassie that. He was just too busy for girls during the crisis, he told her.

He was polite, and treated the girl the same way he'd treated the other women on his tour of the units. When he collected his notes, he thanked her for her cooperation and moved on to the next unit.

Gossip about the police car caught up with him eventually. The man who answered the door and let him in was worried and asked him about the avalanche.

"What avalanche? I've been doing my inventory all morning. You know more about it than I do."

The man shook his head. "I don't know much. What I've heard is that a wall of snow came down off of Swan Mountain and piled up all the way across the highway to Frisco. Now, the only way out is over Hoosier pass toward Alma and Freeplay."

Will felt a shock go through him.

"Do you know if Summit High School was affected? That sounds like its location, and a bunch of refugees are sheltering in those buildings."

The man shook his head. "I don't know a thing. Nobody said anything about the school."

Will could barely keep him mind on his task. *Mr. Winslow was taken to the hospital just over a mile around the bend from there toward Frisco. Kelly might have been sent to the school if the hospital had no room for her.*

He tried to concentrate on his job, but it was hard.

...

Three units later, it got a lot harder.

The big, black-haired guy snarled at him when Will knocked on his door. It was the same guy who'd caused the problems before.

"What do *you* want?"

"I'm Will Parker, the manager's son. I'm inventorying the owner's closets of the condo units."

"Not my unit!"

Will felt his heart go thump. But he was in no mood do back down.

"No, sir. All units have to have their owner's closets checked." He glanced at his sheet for the man's name.

"Mr. Baxter, it won't take more than a few minutes. I've been doing this all morning long."

"Don't bother. There's nothing you want here."

Will blinked. "Sir, have you opened the owner's closet?"

Baxter hesitated. "No, of course not."

"Then I must check for myself." He waved his clipboard. "I need detailed inventory for all the units. Should I bring the manager and have him do it?"

Baxter stood tall, just inches in front of him. "I'm telling you to butt out. I'm staying here, and while I'm here, this is my home. Nobody can just walk in and tell me what to do!"

Will took his pen and started writing. "Baxter refuses—"

The man slapped the clipboard out of his hand and it sailed a few feet down the hallway.

"Hey, what's going on here?" Several of the other doors were open and the next door neighbor glared at Baxter.

Will picked up his clipboard. His wrist stung from the blow.

Keeping a little distance, he spoke again, a little louder so all the neighbors could hear. "Every condo unit has to have its owner's closet checked for any resources we'll need to survive this crisis. Everyone has cooperated thus far. I need you to let me do my job."

Baxter glared at him, and the other people watching the confrontation.

"Okay, hurry it up!"

Will felt the back of his neck tense up as he walked into the unit. The redhead peered fearfully out of the bedroom, watching Will and Baxter enter.

Will pointed at the locked closet. "That's it." He tried not to look around the unit, but one thing was abundantly clear. The place reeked of woodsmoke and a quick glance showed that the wall above the fireplace was darkened with soot.

Don't say a thing. Don't even look at it. Get the inventory and leave.

While the closet door was locked, it was evident that someone, probably Baxter, had tried to pick it. Scrape marks showed on the face of the lock, and the gap between the door and the frame showed that someone had tried to wedge the spring-loaded latch.

But when he opened the door, it didn't look like much of anything was missing. It still had all the usual items, ski boots, skis and poles, extra coats and the usual personal items.

Will wrote down his inventory and locked the door.

"Thank you for your cooperation."

He was out the door before Baxter tried anything else.

The neighbor was watching from his door. "Any problems?"

Will shook his head. "No. I was going to check your unit next, but do you mind if I wait until later?

Avalanche

When Will walked into his father's office, Bob Parker caught his eye and raised his fingers a fraction of an inch.

Will understood. He was recognized, but told to stay quiet for a bit.

The others in the office were Greg the night manager, and Sheriff Thompson.

Thompson was speaking.

"The avalanche came down the whole west slope of Swan Mountain and spilled across the valley at the notch. It took out the buildings on the west side of the highway, the vet's, the women's center and then spilled across taking out the gas station, and half the mobile home park. It covered the Amerigas propane center as well, but that was less disastrous than it could have been because their tanks had already been drained.

Will asked, "Did it reach the high school?"

Thompson looked around to see him in the doorway. "There was some damage, but the main buildings are okay. The avalanche covered the football field."

He turned back to Bob. "It's lucky there were so many people there at the school as it was. We had hundreds of people out on the snow immediately, digging out people who were stranded. Five dead confirmed, but I'm sure there will be more.

"But the reason I came here is to ask if you have any room for more refugees. Over two dozen mobile homes were destroyed and those people are now homeless. Frisco can take some of them, but they're full-to-overflowing with refugees from I-70. We have to find places for some."

Bob frowned. "We're getting very tight on food to feed everyone."

Thompson nodded. "Then I've got some good news as well. This morning the city brought in two full cattle trucks we've parked at the arena on Boreas Pass Road. We paid top dollar for them, although the Park County ranchers will have to sit on the checks for a while. Some fancy restaurant chefs are going to be doing double duty as butchers for a while.

"But the point is that the city is going to be handing out beef, soup bones, and whatever we can salvage to people in town. Places like this lodge will get good portions to handle however many people you're sheltering. It won't last forever, but we've got something to keep people from starving for a while."

"That's good news." Bob looked at the policeman with an appraising eye. "And I assume places like ours which cooperate with the city get put high on the list when resources are handed out?"

Thompson had a smile. "I'm not *saying* that. We have to play fair with the whole town."

Bob looked at his son. "Will, you came in here for something. What is it?"

Will took a breath. "Baxter is burning wood in the gas fireplace in his unit."

The manager frowned. "Are you sure?"

"It's pretty evident. It smells of it. There's soot on the walls. And he tried to keep me out of the unit when I wanted to inventory the owner's closet."

Bob stood up. He turned to Thompson. "We can take about a dozen people, family units preferred. We already have children in the hallways. And would you mind coming with me while I speak to Baxter?"

Thompson put on his serious-policeman face and nodded.

The four of them trudged down the hallway and up the stairs. Will stood back out of the way as his father knocked on the door.

"What is it now?" Baxter opened the door with a scowl.

"I'm Bob Parker, manager of this place. I need to look inside."

Baxter hesitated, looking at the others, eyes focusing on the policeman. "Why do you need to come in? I'm busy. Your boy was just here."

"There was a report of damage to the unit. I need to check on it."

"It's fine."

"I need to come in."

Sheriff Thompson said, "The building manager has every right to inspect the room. The law didn't shut down when the electricity went off. Let him in."

Baxter glared at him. Then, he backed into the unit.

The men filed in. Bob said, "It appears that you've been burning wood in the gas fireplace. I warned everyone against that."

Everyone was staring at the discolored wall above the fireplace. There were wood ashes spilled out onto the floor as well. Someone had hurriedly tried to clean up the evidence.

Baxter said, "It was like that before I came."

Will said, "No, it wasn't. I was here when you were complaining that the gas fire wouldn't start."

Bob explained patiently, "These fireplaces can't handle a wood fire. They're even marked, explaining that. A wood fire risks setting the building on fire. I can't risk having you put us all out in the snow.

"I gave fair warning to all residents here. If you can't follow the rules, I'll have to ask you to pack your things and leave."

Baxter looked at all the faces staring at him. "You can't turn me out into the snow! It was just the one time!"

From the door into the bedroom, the red-haired woman said, "No, he did it every night. He's got a stash of firewood here in the bedroom. He said he didn't have to pay attention to 'house rules.'"

"Beth! Shut your mouth!"

She yelled at him. "I don't care if they turn me out! But I'm not staying with you another minute!"

Baxter straightened up. "I can't leave. My car is in the garage below and the street is blocked. The snowplow hasn't been clearing the side streets."

The manager said, "Your car will be safe here until the streets are cleared, but you have to leave."

Will could hear people out in the hallway. They had attracted a crowd.

Sheriff Thompson said, "The city has a shelter even for those who refuse to follow the rules. The building manager has told you to leave. If you try to stay, you'll be trespassing. I've got handcuffs right here if you want to turn this into an arrest."

The woman, Beth, pulled a bag out and was angrily stuffing her things into it.

Thompson said to her, "I'm juggling several shelters right now. You won't have to stay together."

From the hallway a voice caught Will's attention. Kelly called out, "She can stay with me in my unit, if that's okay?"

Will caught Kelly's eye for just an instant. But she was caught up in the drama.

Bob nodded. "I think that's okay." He turned to Beth. "You can follow the 'house rules', can't you?"

She nodded and looked gratefully at Kelly. Hurriedly, she completed her packing and carried her bag out into the hallway.

Baxter watched, still not moving to comply.

Thompson said, "Better get packing. I don't have all day."

Bob said, "We're staying right here until you're gone. Sheriff, it looks like I'll have room for another family from your refugee list."

"Good to know. Baxter, you look big and strong. How come I've never seen you on the work crews? I can find you a bed, and I can find you a snow shovel as well. How would you like helping clear some of the walkways? As you've noticed, we don't have enough snowplows to keep everything clear."

Baxter grunted and stalked into the bedroom to pack.

Will noticed his father tilting his head. That was permission for him to leave.

He was grateful. He hurried out into the hallway past the others who were watching the events play out. Kelly's room was just a few doors down.

He knocked.

Kelly opened the door and beamed. "Will, it feels like ages!"

Inside, Beth was sitting on the couch, her bag at her feet, crying.

Will pulled her out into the hallway. "What happened? Were you at the avalanche?"

She nodded, eyes wide. "Will, you should have seen it, and heard it! I thought it was the end of the world. The whole side of the mountain came roaring down toward us. Everything Dad ever told me about what to do in an avalanche came back to me, and I couldn't do a thing! I was in a building, not out on my skis. I didn't want to be trapped, but I couldn't run away, not in the deep snow.

"I went to the doorway and held on to the wall. The place shook and I thought it was going to come down on top of me. I could barely stand when it stopped.

"One of the guys grabbed a snow shovel and cleared the entrance way. I got my skis on and helped as well as I could, digging people out of the snow. Will, there were so many people trapped in their trailers! Some were hurt."

She shook her head. "After an hour or so, there were so many helpers digging people out and getting them over to the hospital that I checked in with Dad. The school was crowded before, and I knew I was just taking up space. I had a bed of my own back here, so Dad gave his limited blessing and I skied back home."

"Limited blessing?"

Kelly grinned. "I've got to 'behave myself.'" She called back into the room. "Beth, do you hear that? You're my chaperone."

The woman nodded and waved her acceptance.

You're Needed

Having Kelly follow along on his inventory rounds for the rest of the day was fun. She was better at being friendly with the people than he was and he got to hear her story about the avalanche many times through the day.

Kelly hadn't been there during the first round of food consolidation, so she had a stash of trail mix bags, beef jerky, and assorted protein drinks in her unit. She insisted on getting them donated, along with whatever hadn't gone bad in her refrigerator.

Will savored a stick of beef jerky as Kelly talked to his mother. "I think the TV dinners are all still good. They were frozen and they were still pretty cold when I opened up the refrigerator."

"I'm sure they'll be fine." May Parker looked grateful. "We're not even looking at expiration dates any more. If it's not stinking, someone will eat it."

"Mom? What's going on back there?" He pointed at the east entrance where there appeared to be some people banging on the wall.

"Oh! Some men are building me an outdoor stove. It's going to be right up against the building so the heat can radiate inside. They're hoping it'll help heat the east side of the property, too."

Kelly followed him out as he took a look at the activity.

The first floor east entrance was elevated one floor up on the back side of the building. The parking garage entrance, a hundred feet over was at ground level. But there had been a lot of snow since he'd last come clearing the walkway. Now even the garage entrance was so covered with snow that it'd have to be dug out before it was usable again. Someone had been piling a lot of the snow into a hard-packed ramp, making an easy climb from the covered bridge up to the first floor.

Over near the bridge, snow had been shoveled clear down to the ground, and Will was just a little shocked how deep it had gotten. The walls of snow around that area were six to eight feet tall in places. The covered bridge that crossed Blue River was now a tunnel through the snow.

Three men were rolling one of the boulders up to some others. There were two sides of a six-foot boxed-in area in the making.

He asked, "You're making a fireplace with river rocks?"

All of them were sporting beards, but one man looked like his was there long before the electricity stopped. He nodded, solemnly. "You're the manager's boy, right? Yeah, it's the only building material we have for this job. I know about the problem. We'll be baking them slowly to start."

Will nodded and walked down the ramp to the covered bridge.

Kelly asked, "What's the deal with river rocks?"

Will pointed to the boulders at their feet. "This whole area is made up of boulders dredged up when this was a gold mining area."

"Like that Dredge Boat restaurant?"

"Yeah. The dredge boat dug down to bedrock under the creek, making its own pond as it went. They filtered out all the gold dust and left huge piles of boulders. If you've seen the old photographs, the place looked like a mess before they smoothed everything out and built all the condos, restaurants, and parking lots on top of it.

"But the thing is, although they are solid rock, these boulders have been soaking in the river water for ages. You might not think it, but they have absorbed water. If you heat a river rock, that water will turn to steam. The rock will fracture—splinter into sharp fragments. People have been hurt badly by ignorantly making a fireplace ring out of river rocks and then being caught by the rock splinters when one explodes."

He nodded back at the workmen. "They're going to try to slow-bake the water out of the rocks. Cross your fingers that it works, or will have to haul someone to the hospital over that avalanche rubble."

He glanced through the covered bridge. There was a cleared passageway across the parking lot to the buildings on Main Street. He wished he had time to see what people were doing. His whole world had shrunk to the confines of the lodge.

His mother called, "Will! You're needed."

Kelly nodded. "I've got to go check on Beth anyway. See you later."

He hurried back.

The bus was stopped on the wrong side of the street right in front of the main entrance—not that there was any other traffic on the road. Sheriff Thompson's police car was stopped in front of it with his lights flashing.

Some of the lodge's residents were there, holding the refugee's hands as they stepped down onto the icy road, clutching what little possessions they'd salvaged from their crushed mobile homes.

Greg Turner had the empty units listed, one on each sheet of paper. Will was given a family of five, the Torinos, and he escorted them to their place to stay.

"Come with me. We have to take the stairs—no elevator."

He nodded to the boy, a couple of years younger than him. He'd seen him in school.

"Rick, isn't it?"

"Yeah. You're Will?"

He nodded. "My father runs this place."

When he opened the door, he said, "Come on in. This is your place for the duration. Rick, could you introduce us?"

Will gave them the house rules and the cautionary tale of the guy who got kicked out for building a fire.

Teresa, the youngest at twelve, said, "It's cold in here."

Will nodded. "Yes, and it won't get any better. Did you have heat in your home?"

Jacob, the father, said, "We had a propane heater, but we were almost out of gas."

"Your best bet is to stay bundled up. The main room downstairs and the kitchen area are warmer and many people hang out there. There are plenty of chores to keep you busy—that's how I stay warm. Ask at the main desk if you need more bedding or thicker clothes. There's a limited supply of things we can borrow from the condo owners. What food is available, we share. Everyone has to pull together to survive this."

. . .

On his way back to the front desk, he saw a familiar face, an employee he hadn't seen since the sun flared.

"Ruth! You're back."

The thirty-ish woman smiled, a little tired. "Yes, but not the way I wanted. The avalanche took my place."

"Oh! I'm sorry. Are you okay?"

"Yes, but my mother is in the hospital with a broken arm. When she gets fixed up I'll try to get her over on this side with my sister and me. I hated to leave her in the hospital, but when I heard the lodge was taking in people, I had to get my claim in."

"Well, I'm glad you're back. Dad's been running me ragged since you left." The story wasn't exactly true, but Ruth Dent had been one of those any-task employees that were so valuable at a place like this. He was really glad to see her back.

She nodded. "I'll be checking in with your folks to see what I can do after I get my sister and our other two roommates settled in."

"Take your time. Get your people taken care of."

She smiled and nodded.

The other groups were already taken care of by the time he checked at the front desk. He could hear Sheriff Thompson's voice in his father's office.

Will moved closer.

"We were running low on diesel as it was. Now with the fuel tanks on the other side of the avalanche, as well as two of the snowplows, we're going to be hard-pressed to keep a single lane open all the way over Hoosier Pass."

Bob signaled Will that he could come on in. Thompson nodded his way. "You've heard?"

"Yeah, what you said and details from other people. How long will it take to open the highway again?"

The man sighed. "We're going to have to dig it out. It's too big for a snowplow to shove it aside. We've already got a work crew on our side, but it's less of a disaster for Frisco and they're taking longer to get started." He waved his hand. "A dozen feet deep and five hundred feet wide. How long would it take you to shovel that out?"

Will frowned. "The hospital is on the other side."

Thompson nodded. "Yes. We've got a couple of snowmobiles and we're moving one of the snowcats off the mountain so we can ferry people and small cargo across, but that's it."

Bob asked, "Any detour routes? Say, around the school?"

"Nothing usable. None of those roads have been plowed since the electricity glitched. No, we're just going to have to dig."

"And Swan Mountain Road?"

Thompson shook his head sadly. "Better to wait for spring to melt it out. I'm sure we're going to have to rebuild the road in places. Keystone is off limits for the duration."

Will walked the sheriff back to his car.

"Sir?"

"Yes, Will?"

"What you said to Baxter, about how he hadn't volunteered for any of the work crews—things are easing off here. We've got more workers now. Maybe I should sign up for something."

"You'll have to check with your dad about that. I'm sure you're competent, but cutting trees is a hard, dangerous job. The avalanche crew is going to be doing back-breaking work. I appreciate the offer, but I'd really want a few more years worth of muscle on you before I'd think about it."

Will sighed. "Okay, then. But if you think of something I can do for the city, please let me know."

"I'll do that. But for now, keep this lodge working. That's the best thing you can be doing."

Will watched him drive off, chains clattering on the ice. It had been building up lately—this feeling of being useless. Now with Ruth back, and so many people volunteering to help, he would hardly be missed.

Signs of Life

The inventory job took him three days, and Will was relieved when it was finally done. Some of the owners were there at the door when he knocked. It was much more embarrassing then. Still, they were all in the same boat.

Of course, the next day, Will's father had a job for him, shovel the snow off the decks.

He shoveled and lifted and grunted. *I've got a lot more muscle than the sheriff seems to think. This is all strength training.*

He dumped more snow off the side of the building, taking a moment to watch the snowplow moving through on Park Avenue. It was coming by less frequently, and there was only one lane with some slightly wider spots for people to pass if necessary.

Ski Hill Road, where he was dumping his snow off the first floor deck, was just a white gap between the lodge and the city hall building. He didn't even want to know how deep it was.

The whole town was like that—buildings poking up through the blanket of snow. With the flakes swirling down, it was scenic.

There was signs of life. Park Avenue was plowed. Other people had cut pathways through the snow—more like WWI trenches than cleared sidewalks. Off on Main Street, he could see someone at work. It was just scoops of snow arcing out of a trench. He couldn't see the worker.

How long before they bite the bullet and roof it over? That's what happened during the historic Big Snow—a network of tunnels connected the buildings. He'd just lay down some plywood and let the snow cover it—if he had that much plywood.

I'm sure we don't have more than a sheet or two, and the hardware store is probably closed. Still, that would keep the fresh snow out.

There was a flicker of motion out of the corner of his eye.

Up on the second floor, Kelly was waving out the window.

He nodded, and flashed his wide-spread gloved hand twice. Ten more minutes.

He bent to the work with more effort, trying to clear as much snow as he could in a short time.

A few minutes later, he was dusting the snow off his jacket and greeting Kelly and Beth at the entrance.

"I can smell the beef stew. Is it time to eat yet?" Kelly asked.

He pulled off his gloves and stuffed them in his pocket. "Sounds good to me."

...

The crowd was larger than normal. Word had spread about the fresh beef and everyone wanted a taste. Will asked the Kelly to hold his place in line and made a dash to pick up a pail of water from the utility barrel they kept in the kitchen where the water would stay warm.

He carried it to his family's unit and hurriedly stripped off his coat, took a quick swipe with the wash rag to clean off a little. He dumped the rest in the toilet tank, and since there was enough to flush, he took advantage of that as well.

In a fresh shirt (not that there'd been any laundry since this had started), he put his jacket back on and hurried back to the line.

Beth muttered, "Next time, comb your hair."

Will brushed his fingers through his mop and grinned. It was the first time he'd heard the woman talk since she'd yelled her parting at Baxter. Kelly seemed to be getting along with her okay, and that was all he really cared about.

The chairs were all taken, so bowls in hand, they sat against the wall close enough to the fireplace to get some radiated warmth. Will's bowl was actually a squarish storage container, so he could see the chunks of beef and the occasional corn kernel and potato bit of the same size through the transparent sides. He wondered if those came from one of Kelly's TV dinners.

But it was good—really good—considering how bland the food had gotten.

Beside him, Kelly sighed. "Much better than the soup they served at the high school."

Beth nodded but didn't really talk much. Will mentioned the new people that had arrived and pointed out the Torino family still waiting in line. He saw Ruth Dent and a woman who looked just like her, probably her sister, working the serving line, scooping out the stew into all the makeshift bowls. The Torino's all were carrying their own bowls. Most of the people brought their own dishes from their units.

They washed out their bowls in one of the big black water barrels, as clean as they could. One of his tasks later would be to carry Jerry-cans of the dirty water up to units and offer flushing water to those than needed it. Many families took care of that themselves, but his father made it a point to offer the service for those groups where the fathers were coming back from an exhausting day on the work crews.

Kelly asked, "I wondered about the drains. Won't the pipes freeze up?"

"Probably the clean water tap will have problems when they get the water flowing again. But we're melting snow in those white barrels over there for our clean source and from what I hear, as long as we keep pouring reasonably warm water down the sink, that and with the flushing water going to the main sewer lines should keep them above freezing."

It occurred to him that the downstream waste water treatment plant was just on the other side of the avalanche. He mentally crossed his fingers that the main pipes weren't affected.

"Greetings!" There was a gray-haired man with glasses, his shoulders covered with snow, pulling a foldable wagon behind him. "Sorry to interrupt your meal, but I'm selling books. Cash only, sorry."

Several people moved closer to pull aside the plastic sheet that covered the books. As soon as the covers came to light there was excitement in the air.

"Jenny! Run upstairs and get my purse!"

Kelly and Will edged closer. She whispered, "I could really use a good book right now."

Sadly, Will realized he wouldn't have time—not with his constant chores.

Kelly rummaged through the titles, then snatched up one with a bare-chested, winged man on the cover. "Um, Will, could you . . . ?" She fished out her room key.

He nodded. "Where?"

"Red leather pouch in the dresser. Top drawer."

He hurried up to get it. With the centrally-located elevator down, he had to run the long corridor down to the north end to get to the stairs. Strangely, with two girls now living in that room, it was much tidier than it had been before. Did they do house work as they chatted?

He found the bag and hurried it down. The book-lovers had found each other and there were several intense conversations going on, with promises to loan books out, once they'd been read.

Kelly dug out her bills and paid. The bookseller was professional, handing out receipts, giving correct change, and promising to come by again soon.

Will asked, "What's your route?"

He said, "This is the first time I've tried this, but there should be a complete route now. I'll go south on Park as far as the Village, or until I run out of books, and then cut back to the tunnel on Main. My store is on the second floor, luckily."

"There's a tunnel?"

"In places, yes."

There was a book Will looked for, but didn't see—a history of Summit County. There had been a section that talked about the Big Snow of 1898-9. He'd read it once a couple of years before. He supposed somebody had it.

After the bookseller departed out the front entrance, Kelly said, "I've been meaning to read this for a while. No time like the present." She smiled at Beth. "I'll share it with you when I'm done."

Beth shook her head. "I'm a little soured on big strong men who make your heart flutter when they smile at you."

Will didn't say anything. *I guess she didn't start out dating a jerk. I wonder what set him off?*

Kelly said, "I can't wait to get started on this." She already had it open on page three.

"Do you have candles? I know I'm out."

She shook her head. "I know I've got a fresh charge on my rechargeable flashlight. I'm willing to make the sacrifice."

"When did you charge it?"

"At the high school. They've got access to solar power, but just for about an hour a day. Or they did. I don't know if the avalanche took out the power lines. I know I passed the solar arrays when I skied here. They're almost even with the snow. I bet they'll be covered before too long."

Will nodded. He'd seen them from the bus many times. He just wished the lodge could share some of that juice. Sadly, with the constant overcast, there just wasn't enough power to go around, he realized that. She was probably right about them getting buried as well, unless someone went out there every day and swept them off.

Will walked the girls back to their unit and said goodbye.

He wondered if there were any final chores for the day. By habit, he went back to check at his father's office.

Bob nodded when he walked in. "Will, close the door and sit down." He wasn't smiling.

Will frowned and did as he was told. "What's up?"

The man fidgeted with the pen in his hand. "Will, we've got a tough situation here, with everyone just having to make do to get by. Everyone is having to make sacrifices. People are working together to make sure we survive."

He snapped the pen down on the surface. "When the power comes back, when they clear the streets and there's gas at the gas stations, when these people get in their cars and drive home—that's when there's going to be a lot of finger-pointing.

"I'll be judged for how I've handled this situation. Did I take care of the people properly? Did I protect the owner's units and their possessions? Did I do everything within my power to keep this place intact, ready to return to normal business?

"I honestly fear that I'll be out of a job come spring, or whenever we thaw out."

"Dad, people think you're doing a great job."

He shook his head. "There will be lawsuits. Baxter might sue because I kicked him out. The owner of that unit might sue because of the smoke damage. The condo owner's association won't be happy with that outdoor fireplace I'm letting them build.

"But, Will." He looked him straight in the eyes. "I *don't* want Sam Winslow raising a stink because my son seduced his daughter while he was in the hospital!"

Will was shocked. "Dad! Nothing like that has *remotely* happened! We're *always* out in the public when we're together. I mean ...." He was at a loss for words.

His father nodded. "I didn't think it had. Still. You're in and out of her unit all the time. I can't keep an eye on you during the day. Believe me, people are watching you two. They're starved for entertainment. Of course they're going to gossip."

Will shook his head sullenly. "You've got it all wrong. I'd like to get to know Kelly better, but this—nothing like this is happening!"

Not Even

Will woke with a headache and a need to fill his canteen from the tank in the kitchen. Of course, as soon as the cook on duty saw him, she had him go shovel clean snow for the water supply.

This is my life. I'm the go-do-it guy. I can't do anything on my own time—I don't have any time of my own.

The idea of joining one of the work crews seemed ever more appealing. People knew those guys worked hard and they got to go ahead in the food line, and people like him did extra chores for them.

I work every bit as hard, but what I do is invisible. I've always been here to pick up the slack.

He had to face it. For the duration, he'd be slave labor, with no time for himself. Forget having time with Kelly—even if her father came back and gave his blessing. Dad was too concerned with appearances.

...

It was a little later in the day, after sorting the trash. He was grateful that there were no stores open, and thus no fresh cardboard boxes and packaging trash to deal with. Still people threw things down the trash chutes and stuff built up down at the garage level. It was one of his jobs to make sure nothing valuable got trashed and to bundle up the rest of it. One of these days, someone would have to figure out what to do with all the trash. They couldn't even open the garage door—not unless he did some serious snow clearing outside.

Regular trash pickup had stalled. The same problem existed all over town, he guessed. Some of it could be burned, but there was always the rest.

He was wondering about what the long-term solution would be, when he saw Rick intensely playing a game on his cell phone, leaning against the wall in the hallway.

"Hey, Rick. Did you charge your phone off solar before you came?"

Rick's frown turned up into a grin. "No." He played another few seconds and then hit pause.

He pulled out a gadget almost the same size as his phone from his jacket pocket and plugged it into his phone. A handle folded out and he cranked like mad.

"I can get about ten minutes of play time when I crank the generator for fifteen. It's been a lifesaver."

"Wow. Is there any chance I could get my phone charged?"

He'd been sullenly ignoring the rare moments of sunlight, knowing that there was no way to take photos even if he could get his telescope set up in time. But if he could charge his phone, then he just might be able to take a rare picture. And not just sunspots either.

The last time he read about the Big Snow, there had been a comment that there was little documentation of that time since the newspaper had run out of supplies. Maybe he should take pictures of this event. They might be valuable sometime in the future.

Rick frowned thoughtfully. "I really don't want to let it out of my sight."

"That's wise. But if I sat here?"

He shrugged. "I suppose."

"I'll have to get my phone. I'll be back in a jiffy."

"Take your time, I'll still be cranking. I don't want the game to go blank right when it's getting good."

...

Will got used to cranking the thing.

Rick gave him tips. "Turn your brightness down and don't just turn it off—power it all the way down. And leave it in airplane mode, so it won't waste power looking for cell signal and Wi-Fi."

Will knew most of the tips for saving power on his cell phone, but it didn't hurt to be reminded.

He got his phone up to 25% charged before he had to go back to work. He snapped a picture of Rick intently focused on his game, and then powered his phone down.

. . .

"How is the fireplace coming?" Will asked. The construction looked complete. There was a heavy metal grate propped over the fire, just perfect for cooking.

The man in charge nodded, tossing another log into the fire. "We're getting some fractures in the rocks, but it actually makes the walls more stable. Better than a bunch of round boulders stacked on top of each other."

"Can I take some pictures?"

"Go right ahead, but don't get too close. Every now and then we'll hear another crack."

Will took his pictures and then looked over at the covered bridge. On a whim, he walked through, getting shots of the walkway on the other side. Someone had shoveled it recently. The walls on either side were taller than his head.

Time to roof this over. But it was someone else's task.

"Will!"

He sighed. Someone was calling for him. He turned back.

. . .

"There you are!" Kelly sat down beside him, holding her bowl. He'd found a comfortable spot in the glow of the new fireplace. "I haven't seen you all day."

He sipped the broth. "Yeah. I've been busy."

She grinned. "The book was great. I thought for sure you'd come by and borrow it."

He didn't quite meet her eye. "Sorry. I'm afraid your place is off limits for a while."

She frowned. "What? Why?"

"Dad's orders."

Her eyes were hard and angry. "Explain."

He sighed. He hadn't wanted to meet up with her because it was hard to explain. He'd worked on the words in his head all day.

"My father made the case that when the power comes back on, he'll be judged for how well he cared for the lodge and its inhabitants. Including the reputation of a teenage girl left without her father."

Her anger was written all over her face. "That's ridiculous. I'm going straight to the office and clear this up. We've done nothing—"

"Don't. Without making a big deal of it, just take a look at how many people are watching us right now. Dad said we're the closest thing to a soap opera these people have. I'll probably get another lecture for talking to you now."

Her mouth dropped open and she took another spoon from her bowl and glanced around.

"This is ridiculous. He can't tell me who I can talk to." But her voice had dropped and she was aware of people watching and listening.

"I know that. I also know he's not wrong about some things. We're in strange times and ... social norms are skewed funny."

She glared at her bowl of stew. "I know. I was just relishing the change. No dad to ask me about how I spent my day. No home-school task to bother with. Even a new girlfriend to chat with in the dark hours.

"I am *not* going to take kindly to some guy who's not my father checking up on me." She looked up at Will. "What do you think about this?"

He stirred his spoon in his bowl. "I'm not happy. I was really looking forward to spending more time with you." He half smiled. "Maybe even read your book.

"But right now Dad is in charge, and I can't see sneaking around his back when we weren't even...."

She sighed. "Yeah. Not even." She concentrated on her stew for a bit.

She finished it off and with a clatter of her spoon in the bowl, she said, "You can tell your father that I'm going to talk to whoever I want to talk to. I'll share my meals with any person I want. So expect me do just whatever I want to do. You may have to toe the line, but I don't!"

She got up and walked over to rinse out her bowl.

Will ate slowly, not staring at her, but aware of when she left.

A few minutes later, he finished as well, and when he was done, he looked around and waved.

"Hey Rick."

The kid nodded, the frown on his face not lifting. But he handed him the charger. Will sat down beside him and cranked until his arm ached.

Another guy came by. "Hey, what're you doing?"

He was Joe Hester. He also had a dead phone. Rick sighed and then gave him the rules. Joe chatted and watched Rick's game while Will finished. Joe was a stranded tourist from Texas.

"I was getting pretty good at snowboarding—at least not falling down quite as much. But now, stuck here, with the slopes closed, I was going crazy without even my games to keep me busy."

With a fully-charged phone, Will said, "Thanks." He handed back the charger and left the guys debating which games were best. Will suspected that with Rick's charger, the boy was going to become much more popular. He hoped so. The kid had a perpetual frown on his face.

Will went out the front entrance and took a few night shots of the snow coming down, detailing the narrow lane plowed on Park Avenue.

Careful to power down his phone, he sighed, picked up the snow shovel and made sure their entrance could be accessed from the road. The only cars on the road seemed to be the police, and the pickups that delivered firewood and food supplies and carried the work crews to their destinations, but he wanted them to have it as easy as possible.

When he finally went to his place, his father was there at the kitchen table working on some papers by the light of a kerosene lantern.

"I saw Miss Winslow eating with you earlier."

"Yeah Dad. She sought me out. I gave her the bad news and she didn't take it well."

"Oh?"

"Yes, something about not willing to have anyone messing with her life other than her father."

Bob nodded. "Not unexpected. You just make sure that you do what's proper."

Will grunted and then went on to bed. He really didn't want to have that talk again.

Harris Street

When Will struggled from dreamland to breathe in the chill air of his bedroom, he had to face reality.

While the dream had been exciting and nearly messy, the truth of the matter is that Kelly never had even approached being that close and sweaty with him. It was all a fantasy triggered by his father's meddling. There was no evidence at all that she'd be that willing to get any more intimate than amiable conversation. The details were rapidly fading, but he remembered the intense parts.

And if my dream is any indication, there are plenty of ways a couple could find a bit of privacy, even if a bedroom was off limits.

As he dressed for the day, he nodded. Just like in his dream, it wouldn't be hard to sneak down to the parking garage and spend some time in the back seat of the Winslow's car. It was pitch black down there, and hardly anyone went to the cars since the power went out and the garage door was blocked. It might even be safe to heat up the car to a comfortable temperature in spite of the signs warning people against letting their cars idle in the enclosed space.

He sighed. *Dad could be right. I might not have a lot of resistance if the right temptation came along.* He could see that temptation smiling at him in his imagination.

Concentrate on your job.

He joined the men getting their lunch pails before they caught their rides. He settled for biscuits soaked in beef broth.

Mrs. Kirk gave him an extra. "Better savor these. The flour is running low."

He nodded, and began his morning chores.

...

A couple of hours later, the pickup with firewood and food arrived a second time.

Will was close to the door. "What's up? We weren't expecting a delivery."

The driver shrugged. "I was told to drop it here. The Harris Street Association would pick it up."

Will nodded. "Okay then, let's unload and I'll let them know when they show up."

They had a half-cord of wood and beef bundled up in a sheet. Will stacked everything there at the entrance under the canopy where the snow wouldn't collect on it. The driver thanked him and drove off.

Fifteen minutes later, Terry Johnson, a friend of his at school walked up, coming through the covered bridge, towing a wagon. People moved out of his way as he came up to the registration desk.

"Is this River Mountain Lodge?"

"Hey, Terry." Will waved from across the room. "Are you from Harris Street?"

Terry looked relieved. "Yes. I got lost in the passages. Took a wrong turn. There was supposed to be a delivery?"

"Yeah, I've got it over here at the front entrance."

He looked very relieved. "Great! I was afraid they'd give it away to someone else."

Will led him to the entrance.

Terry looked panicked. "What's all this?"

"Beef and firewood. Isn't that what you wanted?"

Terry looked at his wagon. "Yes, but... I didn't realize it was going to be this much. I'll never be able to haul it all back."

Will looked at his wagon. It was a foldable cloth and metal wagon. If they loaded the whole half-cord of firewood, assuming it fit, it'd collapse the framework.

"Let me check with my father. Go ahead and start loading what you can."

He quickly got permission to help. He got one of lodge's luggage carts with big wheels and started loading firewood. Together, they loaded half the wood. Terry's wagon carried the food bundle as well.

Will smiled. "Okay, lead the way."

By the time they got to the covered bridge, they'd had to stop twice to re-stack wood that had fallen, but it wasn't too bad.

Terry asked, "How's it going at the lodge. It looked crowded."

"Oh, not too bad. It is crowded down on the first floor where the fireplace is always burning. For some people, the only heat is what drifts down the hallway or what energy people burn themselves. Now that we've got all the windows sealed and covered with drapes and blankets, the rooms aren't too bad, as long as you keep wearing your jacket."

Terry nodded. "Harris is just a bunch of houses. People were getting their own wood from the stockpiles at the parking lots, but once they stopped plowing the streets and the snow got deep, it was too difficult for single families to keep up. When the city announced that the beef was available and that they would deliver to multi-family groups along the highway, people got together and organized our own group."

"Is this new?"

Terry grinned. "Yeah. When I heard there was a passageway all the way to your lodge from the library, I volunteered to get the first load. Honestly, I thought it would just be the food."

Will tugged hard to get over an irregular patch. "This is fine, so far."

Terry frowned. "Hmm. There might be curbs and steps."

Will sighed. "Okay, we'll get through it someway."

Actually, the curbs had changed into ramps by the packed snow and the steps were only indoors and they managed by lifting the wagon and the luggage cart one at a time, easing them over the obstruction. The really hard part was when they got past Main Street and the grade got steeper. Most of the path was shortcuts through buildings, with passageways and tunnels crossing the streets.

Will paid attention whenever they went through a tunnel. Yes, there were a few places roofed over by plywood. There was even one stretch that had an archway of packed snow, just like you'd imagine the Eskimos doing it. One stretch caught his attention and he took a breather to look it over.

Someone had cut tree branches, draped them over with what looked like brightly-colored ladies summer dresses, and then soaked them down to freeze. Once it was rigid, it was put in place as a roof over the trench.

Will wondered how much snow it would support. In any case, he approved of the creativity. He pulled out his phone and snapped some pictures.

"You charged your phone?"

"A kid at the lodge has one of those hand-crank chargers."

"That's nice. I used the car charger until my father called it quits. He was afraid I'd run the battery down."

Will felt stupid for forgetting about that option. He never traveled by car, so he didn't have a car charger. He bet other people at the lodge had tried it, though.

"Hey, there's Terry!" A couple of guys were coming down the trench.

"Hey guys." Terry paused. "Wanna help us?"

They had been searching for him, since he'd been late getting back to the library. With their help, they quickly delivered the load.

"Thanks for your help, Will is it? It's our fault we didn't send more people. We'll get the rest of the load."

Will considered and then nodded. "As long as my cart makes it back to the lodge."

"We can do that."

Will waved goodbye to Terry, who was preparing to head back with helpers.

This is my chance to wander around a little. He'd seen a half-dozen side branches on the way uphill to Harris Street. He wanted to see more of the half-buried version of Breckenridge.

...

Rather than head back down hill, he took one of the paths south, following Harris Street. It was a narrow path, and he quickly realized it wasn't covered over because it wasn't a trench down to the ground level. From the sounds as he walked, some of the path was over buried bushes and cars.

I guess it was cut later, after the road was buried. They just took a short cut.

But he didn't like walking over cars. When it all thawed, someone was going to be upset about the dents.

He took a side branch that went so steeply downhill that someone had cut wide steps in the snow. There was a turn and abruptly, the path ended at a door. Timidly, he knocked.

"Don't bother to knock!"

He entered, and a couple of people looked his way.

"Sorry, just passing through. Is there an exit downhill?"

"Sure, just keep going." The place was a house that had long ago been converted into a clothing store. It looked like, for the duration, someone had closed up shop and was now using it as their house. Timidly, Will kept on walking.

On the other side was a T-junction. He turned left.

After several twists and turns, and one dead-end, he recognized the fudge and ice-cream shop—not that there was anything sweet left on the shelves. He stepped out into a tunnel that had to be on Main Street. He turned north, more confident of his bearings. He passed people in the tunnel. Some were carrying candles for light. His flash, when he took pictures, caught some peoples' attention.

In places, the roof was thin enough that some light leaked through from the daylight above. In other places, he noticed soot marks on the snow.

Abruptly, there was a branch to the south, and a sheriff's deputy was pinning up a sheet to a poster board fixed to a lamp post. Will turned on his cellphone light.

The man looked up. He looked familiar, sitting behind a desk at the sherrif's office, collecting complaints.

"What do you have there?" Will asked.

"Just a revised schedule for the work crews."

Will took a look. There were other notices as well, all hand-written. Most of what they said he'd been told directly by Thompson. They told of the meat deliveries and where firewood could be obtained. There was an announcement of the Swan Mountain avalanche and the request for people to help dig it out.

The man was watching him as he read.

Will looked his way.

"You're that kid from River Mountain Lodge, aren't you?"

Will glanced at his name tag.

"Yes, Deputy Curtis. I recognize you from that first day."

The man chuckled. "Yeah. What a nightmare! Thompson talks about you."

Will winced. "Good or bad?"

"Oh, good, mostly. He wasn't happy you went up on the mountain on your snowmobile."

"He told me."

"What are you doing over here?" the man asked.

"Exploring the new map of Breckenridge. I had to help the Harris Street Association get their delivery and I'm just taking a different route home. I get a little stir-crazy stuck in the lodge all the time. I tried to sign up for a work crew, but the sheriff turned me down."

"Hmm. I'll keep that in mind."

"Yes, anything to help. I'm flexible."

"Well, I've got to go walk my route. Have to let the people know the law enforcement officers are still on the job, even when the whole place is buried."

Will waved and moved on. Another few steps and he found the path he'd taken earlier. There were ruts in the footpath showing the wheel tracks. He turned toward home.

Recharging

Several things came together in his head when he realized his cell phone was down to twenty percent and he needed to charge it up again. He hated to constantly pester Rick for his gadget. He already owed him.

"Dad, I've got an idea. Tell me what you think."

Bob Parker listened his plan with a slight frown. Then he sighed. "Okay, if you think that'll work. You're probably right about people wasting their gas."

Will smiled. He could rig a charging station for himself, but as long as Dad approved, why not share the wealth?

"Great. I'll try to have it ready by supper."

He went out and although he looked for Rick, he didn't see him. He saw Joe, playing on his cell phone and asked him where the guy was, but he didn't know either.

Will went down the stairs and into the dark parking garage. He listened for a moment, but didn't hear anyone. Risking the last of his phone's battery, he lit up the screen and made his way to the storage room. He quickly found the hefty booster battery they used to jumpstart people's cars when they had let their battery run down. Normally, he had to plug it into the wall socket to top it up, but that was no longer possibe.

He carried it over to the Subaru Forester that his parents owned and popped the hood. When he connected the booster battery there was a spark and he checked the little bar graph display. You weren't really supposed to charge the booster from the car, usually the other way around, but it worked.

Dad rarely let him use the car for anything, so he was pleased with himself as he sat down on the cold upholstery and started the engine. It fired up quickly and he confirmed that there was plenty of gas in the tank and the engine was running smoothly.

He double-checked the booster battery, happy that the voltage was climbing up past thirteen volts. He sat back in the driver's seat and turned the heater up, relishing the feel of hot air.

It would be perfect if Kelly was here with me. If this is a success, then I'll have to come down here every so often to charge up the booster battery again. Maybe I could invite her.

It was a pleasant vision, but it would also be the quickest way to have his father shut down his idea for a public charging station.

The headlights had come on automatically with the engine running. His eyes were attracted to some trash on the next aisle over between two cars. He sighed. Habit wouldn't let him ignore it. He got out and carried the sack over to the trash. It was someone's long-stale McDonalds leftovers, and the smell was enough to make him hungry.

It's going to be a whole new world when the power comes back on and we rediscover all the treats we missed.

...

Rick saw him coming down the hallway. "Were you looking for me?"

Will knelt down beside him. "Yeah. Could you write up the checklist on how to save power on your cell phone? Clear penmanship, and simple enough so adults can understand it?"

"Um. I suppose. If you give me pen and paper. What's this about."

"I'm working on something to keep your hand-crank charger from wearing out." He whispered the details. "I'll reveal it at supper."

Rick looked amused. "Clear enough for adults?"

"Yeah. I'll post it next to the charger." Will was pleased to see the boy's interest. Anything was better than seeing Rick constantly leaning against the wall, frowning down at some game.

...

"Where have you been all day?" Kelly looked at him seriously. "Are you avoiding me?"

He smiled. "Nope. Other projects. All will be revealed in a few minutes."

As people started lining up for the evening meal, Will walked over to the front desk and pulled out the booster battery from where he'd concealed it. He set it down on one of the round tables with a thud.

People were watching as he plugged his cell phone into the charging cord connected to one of the USB jacks on the battery.

"Hey, people! I went for a tour down town this afternoon and took some pictures. If you want to see how the rest of the town is coping, come look at my cellphone."

He sat down and displayed his photos as some people gathered around. Not all were willing to give up their place in line, but for the people close by at the table, he stepped through the pictures he'd taken, commenting on what he'd seen.

Kelly was right beside him. He gave her a quick wink, but otherwise talked to everyone equally.

"It looks like the whole town has collected into 'neighborhoods' just to take advantage of the city's rules about food and firewood delivery. Expect more people to come through the lobby like those guys from Harris Street did today.

"The route from the covered bridge through the building to the front entrance is now a public thoroughfare just like the streets and sideways were before the snow got so deep. It's a convenient route some people use to get to the highway where the pickups can deliver their goods."

Kelly poked his elbow. "Show them the solar flare. Not everyone has seen it."

There were a few assenting voices, so he flipped through his pictures and found the sunspot with the white hotspot. There were a few questions about the pictures, but many people had already seen them.

"What I want to know is can I borrow a charge from your battery there?" The gray-haired lady said, "I've got hundreds of Kindle books loaded on my phone and now is the time to read them."

Will smiled. "I'm glad you asked. Yes, the battery will be sitting at the front desk. There's two USB ports you can plug your cord into. If you have a car-charger handy, it can go into this cigarette lighter port here.

"Rick Torino has written up a handy guide on how to preserve battery life on both iPhone and Android phones. Make sure you follow his instructions. I'll recharge the booster battery when it goes dead, but we still only have limited gasoline to recharge it."

Bob Parker, listening in on his son's words, added. "And I'd like to restrict people going down to the parking garage without letting us know. There's no light at all down there and you could fall and maybe nobody would find you for hours."

Will showed off his pictures to a new set of people, each sipping from their bowls, then he set up the charger at the front desk and Rick's set of instructions on the poster board behind it. Several people scrambled to charge their phones.

Kelly sniffed. "I should have asked to be first in line."

...

Will got his serving and found a place to sit. Kelly settled down beside him.

"So, now that your phone is charged, are you going to try to take more sunspot pictures?" she asked.

He winced. "I suppose. Has there been any sunlight?"

"Oh, yes! Twice yesterday."

"I didn't notice." He wondered where he was at the time. Maybe in the garage, or possibly in the tunnels.

"Are you giving up your science fair project?"

He sighed. "I guess. I don't think there will be a science fair this year. Are they even holding school?"

"One of the teachers was trying to do mini-classes when I slept at your high school, but there wasn't more than a half-dozen people there."

Out of the corner of his eye, Will glimpsed Sheriff Thompson walking into his father's office.

"Kelly, excuse me. I've got check on something." He set down his half-empty bowl and hurried over to the office.

The men looked up as he entered. Thompson smiled. "I wondered when you'd show up."

Will blinked. "I was just curious. It's so late."

"It's okay. I knew this was your meal time. If I come by for a chat at meal time, I might get a taste of your mother's cooking."

His father said, "Don't tease him. He knows something's up."

The policeman shrugged. "Well, it's nothing critical, and your dad hasn't made up his mind yet."

Will could see the smile. Thompson was playing with him. Will sighed. "Oh, well. I thought it might be something important."

"I suppose it is *important*. Honestly, I don't have time for anything that isn't at least important these days. Mostly, however, it's *urgent* or *critical*."

Thompson paused again. "But you talked to Deputy Curtis earlier. And it occurred to us that you might help us with one of those important tasks that we haven't had time to deal with."

Will was suddenly alert. "I'll help where I can."

"It's up to your dad. Let me explain. I'm not just the sheriff for downtown Breckenridge. I'm a Summit County official and I should be touring the whole county, helping everyone. The avalanche has me confined to the Breckenridge side, but I do have deputies working on the north side. But now that all the side roads are shut down, there are a lot of people in the extended area that are isolated. With no phones and impassable roads, there are people who could be in critical need that we don't even know about.

"Alternatively, a lot of those seasonal homes are empty. Either because they got out early, or they just weren't occupied when the solar storm hit.

"Your father mentioned how you inventoried all the owners' closets in the lodge. Well, we need to do something similar with those houses. How many of them have stocked pantries? We're desperate for food. We need to find out what resources are available here in this valley, because lives depend on them.

"If there were officers and snowmobiles to spare, the police and my deputies would take care of it. But we don't. Our people are all busy with existing tasks and our snowmobiles are all spoken for.

"Curtis reminded me that you guys have one. What do you think about visiting those remote houses? Offer the city's aid if they need it. Inventory the resources if the houses are empty."

Will looked at his father, who was looking at him.

A New Start

"Excuse me?" Kelly poked her head around the door. "Will, you left your supper behind." She handed him his bowl.

Then she turned to his father. "Oh, I don't mean to interrupt, but I meant to let you know that I'm going to see Dad at the hospital in the morning."

Bob frowned. "The avalanche—"

She smiled and waved her hand. "Oh, that doesn't stop me. I'm a cross-country skier from way back."

"Um. I'm sure that's okay. How long will you be gone? Or are you—"

She sighed. "Don't know for sure. Depends on how well Dad is doing and all. I may be back before you miss me, but I didn't want you to worry if I showed up missing. I've told Beth."

Will noticed that she didn't look his way. She just wanted his father to know.

Bob nodded. "Okay then, but if you have any problems, be sure to get a message to us."

"I'll do that." And then she was off.

Will took a sip of his stew and then turned back to Officer Thompson. "It will take some time to dig the snowmobile out from the storage shed, but that's just more snow shoveling, and I'm good at that."

Thompson smiled. "Is she your girlfriend?"

Will shook his head. "Not if Dad has his way."

The sheriff looked at Mr. Parker. "Oops. Sorry I mention it."

There didn't seem to be any question about Will's permission to do the job. They discussed the details. Once he got the snowmobile running,

Thompson would have maps and other documentation for him at the sheriff's office. Will's father suggested that he could keep the snowmobile at the lodge and they could fuel it by siphoning gas from some of the cars in the parking garage. It was a day job, and he could be home for supper and sleep in his own bed.

When Thompson left and Will went to wash his bowl, Beth came close enough to whisper, "Are you trying to break up with Kelly?"

He blinked and glanced around at who might be listening. People with lit up cell phones were attracting a lot more attention that he was.

"No! It's just my parents wanting me to keep my distance."

"Then you'd better tell her that. She's confused." Then she walked away.

Will sighed. *Like I could go knock on her door and talk. That's precisely what I've been forbidden to do.*

But he was going to have a big day tomorrow. He walked the hallways, just in case she was out and about, but he didn't see any sign of her.

His mother was in their place when he came home.

"Oh, that Winslow girl delivered the snowmobile suits. She apologized for keeping them so long."

Will saw the folded bundle. "Okay, good." He'd just missed her then. *How did she know I needed the snowmobile gear. Did she overhear our conversation in the office?*

Not that it mattered. He would have told her himself if he'd seen her. And she was leaving tomorrow to go back to the hospital.

I don't want to think about that now. I need to get some sleep.

. . .

Will woke early and dressed for a long day in the snow. The one-piece heavily insulated overalls that Kelly had returned were welcome. He didn't even zip up the front at first.

He begged a lunch pail, explaining the new job he was on. Mrs. Kirk added a bag of beef dice, her homemade jerky. Not every cut of beef that was delivered was perfect for stew, so the cooks were experimenting with finding the best way to use every bit of it.

He borrowed one of the snow shovels. He knew there was already one at the storage shed, but he'd have to dig out the shed to reach it. Shovel over his shoulder like a rifle, he headed out the front entrance and started hiking down the plowed highway. He'd rather not try to wade through the deep snow and he wasn't at all sure the maze of trenches and tunnels extended as far at the storage sheds. In fact, thinking about it, he was confident they weren't.

Every piece of that maze was maintained by somebody. His part was the front entrance of the lodge and the trench between the rear entrance and the covered bridge, although his father would probably handle that while he was gone. Nobody was going to maintain any of the paths that weren't already being used. It was too much work.

He heard the snowplow coming a long way off. Hurriedly, he found a broken down part of the side wall and climbed up out of the way. It was three minutes before the plow came blasting through and nearly buried him in the snow and ice it scraped clear.

He brushed himself off and climbed back down to the road. It was noticeably darker and he could even see hints of the pavement underfoot. He hurried on. He didn't want to run into some police car or delivery truck.

He'd lost track of which side streets he'd passed, but when Park Avenue bent to the east, he knew where he was. Off to the right was the parking lot for City Market and the other shops in that strip mall. It was just a big pile of snow. He could even see that the snow plows had dumped some of the excess snow there. The shops were all deserted and nearly buried with snow. Someone had cut a path up to City Market.

Will nodded. Even with the food all gone, there were sure to be supplies of some kind that could be salvaged from the place. *They'd better take care of the building. Once the electricity comes back on, everyone is going to come here to get supplies.*

Off on the other side, the sheriff's office's parking lot was cleared, with two police cars parked there. Lights came through the windows. Up on the roof, he could see that the solar panels were brushed clear. He guessed they had a battery to collect what power they could and even in this overcast morning light, they had to be getting a trickle of juice.

But that wasn't his destination yet.

Another five hundred feet, leaving the highway as it turned north again and wading through deep snow, nearly swimming through it in places, he reached the storage building.

As he expected, his family's unit was deep in a drift. A couple of the other units looked like they'd been shoveled out, but days ago. It was all white mounds of snow.

He got close enough to bang on the doorway, at least the top of the doorway.

Now, dig.

He bent to the task. It looked overwhelming, but he'd been doing the same sort of excavations since the snow season began. Don't fret about how big the job is. Just choose where to shovel next.

...

He heard the hiss of skis. He looked up, and saw Kelly bank to a stop.

She pushed up her goggles and smile. "I thought I'd find you here."

He rested on his shovel. "So you did overhear the plan."

"Of course! What girl wouldn't snoop on a secret meeting? Bringing your stew was just an excuse to get close."

"So was the plan to visit your father real, or just a tale to get you out on your skis?"

"Oh, it was spur-of-the-moment, but I really am going to go visit my dad. I needed to bring him a supply of double-A batteries for his radio. Part of the deal with living at the lodge is that we keep in touch and I could tell that his signal was getting weaker."

She slipped off her skis and stuck them in the snow. "Do you need any help?"

"Probably, I'll be ready to open the door in a bit. It'll be just like the last time."

She watched as he shoved more of the snow. "My real reason for getting out here is that this seemed to be the only way to talk freely." She looked around at the scene. It was quiet and peaceful. There was no snow falling at the moment, but the clouds looked as if they held more.

Will nodded. "Yeah. It got messed up back at the lodge. I don't know why my father had to make a big deal of it."

She asked, quietly, "I wasn't really sure what you thought about it all."

He shrugged. "I don't want to make a big deal of it either, although ...."

"Although what?"

He concentrated on scraping the snow down at the bottom of the shed's door. "I probably shouldn't admit this, but I have been thinking about you, quite a bit."

She laughed nervously. "Well, I don't mind that. I may not be hunting for romance, but a girl doesn't like to be ignored either."

He nodded, glad he just said he'd been thinking about her, rather than dreaming about her. That might have been too much.

Will dug out the keys and unlocked the shed. The door stuck the first time he tugged at it, but then it came free.

They both went in. It was dark and hard to see until their eyes adapted. Will was rummaging in the clutter at the back.

"What are you looking for?"

"Snowshoes. I could have really used them this morning." He found them and strapped them onto the back.

Kelly patted the cushion. "I remember riding on this. Not the end-all in luxury."

"No, but it got us where we needed to go."

"Yeah."

"Will?"

"Yes?"

"Thanks for rescuing my father. I don't think he would have survived if we hadn't acted."

Will chuckled. "That's what I told my father when he was ready to lower the boom. I'm really surprised he agreed to this new project."

He straddled the seat and said, "Get clear. I'm going to start it up."

She patted him on the shoulder and moved out of the way.

The engine started easily. He checked the gas. Perhaps three gallons. Enough to get started.

Kelly smiled. "I guess I'd better go visit Dad. You've got more work to do."

He reached out, and held her hand, glove to glove. "Thanks for dropping by. It's really great to be able to talk without worrying about what people are thinking."

Ski Hill Road

There were snowmobile tracks at the entrance to the sheriff's office when he drove up. Someone had already been there.

He walked in, stamping his feet to keep from tracking in too much snow.

Deputy Curtis was at a large map of the city and the surrounding area. "I'm glad you made it. Did you have trouble digging out your snowmobile?"

"It wasn't too bad. I saw other tracks?"

"Oh, yes. James Upton from the Village had a snowmobile and volunteered to take part of the job. We're hoping to recruit more people as well."

He pointed to the map. "James took this area, off of Boreas Pass. Pick your area."

Will stared at the map. How about here?" He waved. "Ski Hill Road and the side roads off of it."

Curtis nodded. "That's good. Police are already handling the area up to the Peak 7 lodge, but the road beyond there is snowed in. I've got a city map for you."

"Thanks. I'll need to stop by my place first to top up my gas tank, but then I can get started right away."

Curtis gave him a logbook and a nice sheet that declared that Will Parker was working for the sheriff's department and stated what services the city could provide. His name was hand-written on the form. Probably James Upton had one just like it. "We had electricity for long enough to get this printed and laminated. I'm hoping for some more sun. We've got a generator, but my gasoline budget is very tight."

Will nodded. "When will this snow ever end?"

"I have no idea. I really miss the weather forecasts. All I can do is stare at the clouds. Are you sure the solar flare had nothing to do with the weather?"

"I can't imagine how. It's just a heavy snow year—with no snowplows."

Curtis nodded. "I've got some people digging through the parking lots, looking for diesel-powered cars to siphon from. Something's got to change or we'll even lose the ability to keep the highway open."

"We can still get over Hoosier Pass, right?"

"Yes, but Park County is as hard up as we are. We've sent one car down to Buena Vista and another one toward Denver on Highway 24, looking for someone to ship us diesel, but we haven't heard from either of them yet."

"What's the range on your radios?"

"It really depends on the terrain. We need to send a car down to the avalanche to talk to the police in Dillon and it's best to drive up to the top of Hoosier Pass to talk to Fairplay. I'm missing the big radios that got fried. The car radios weren't really designed for long range communication in the mountains."

...

Sporting his official document like a badge of office, Will drove back to the lodge. His father was waiting for him, with a five-gallon Jerry can of gas to top him up.

Ski Hill Road was right there, so all he had to do was power up the ramp onto the unplowed road and take the hairpin turns up the slope, passing the Peak 8 lodge and then on to Peak 7's buildings. He followed the tracks of a snowcat. There were people living there in the ski-in/ski-out lodges and that was probably their only access to food and firewood. At least, they'd probably started out with more food. Each of the base lodges had big cafeterias designed to serve large crowds of skiers.

He could plainly tell where the earlier plowing had ended. The road beyond the north end of the Peak 7 lodge looked like it had never been plowed. The only hint of a road was the gap in the trees and the plain marking on his map.

He took a deep breath, gunned the throttle and plowed into the deep powder.

It was fun. Snowmobiling had been a family thing, when they had time to take a break. Usually, they went to a place past Copper on Highway 91. He had looked forward to when he could take the snowmobile out by himself and go wherever his whim led.

But... that wasn't today. He kept the machine centered between the trees on either side as the road twisted from side to side.

A power line almost caught him by surprise. As deep as the snow was, the power and utility lines that followed the road were now just a few feet above the snow level. He'd have to watch that carefully. They'd only been strung high enough so that trucks and snowplows could get through. They didn't count on snow this deep.

A roof. He slowed down. He had to visit each and every house. That was the plan.

He eased up into the driveway. It looked deserted. No tracks in the snow. No vehicles.

He turned the key and reached for his snowshoes. Even with them, he sank a bit into the snow.

Knock, knock.

There was no response. *What now? Do I break in?*

He had to get inside if he were going to inventory the assets. He rummaged for a hidden key, scraping snow aside to look for hiding places. After a few minutes, that proved fruitless.

"Break a window maybe?" He didn't like that idea. But Sheriff Thompson had hinted at such extremes.

He tried the doorknob to see if it had any play, and it opened easily. They had left the door unlocked. *Stupid. Try that the first thing next time.*

Will fished out his logbook and on the first page, he noted down the time and the fact that there had been no response to his knock. He looked around.

On the kitchen table was a note:

Paul,

If you show up, we've all gone to the lodge just down the road. The power outage is in its second day and we're not prepared for this. If it lasts much longer, we'll have to go back to Denver. Call us when the phone comes back up.

— Luke and Mary

Will added the information to his logbook, and then rummaged through their pantry. Fifteen minutes gave him a short list of foods, and a one-line summary of other resources. In desperate times it might be worth coming back here with a snowcat to raid the place, but he was just getting started and he was after information, not supplies. A snowmobile wasn't really designed to carry much cargo.

He drew a line on their note and under it, he added the date and:

This house was inventoried by Will Parker, acting for the Summit
County Sheriff's office. Nothing was taken.

Will intended to document everything he did. That's what they agreed on. If he took anything, or damaged the building to gain entrance, he needed to write it all down—an IOU for the county to repay once this was all taken care of. They were on untested legal ground.

Supposedly, necessity was a valid legal defense for otherwise illegal actions, but it was hard to prove. He was acting under the authority of the sheriff's office, so that helped, but he had to be able to document and defend what actions he took, otherwise it was just looting, and that was firmly on the bad side of the line.

After closing the door tightly, he started the engine and moved on.

Almost immediately, he saw a driveway on the right.

There were two houses in sight.

Someone opened the door as he drove up.

Will moved closer and turned off the key. He yelled, "Hey there! I'm Will Parker, working for the sheriff."

He pulled out his laminated sheet and read aloud the offer of services.

The man nodded. "Good to hear. We're planning to tough it out for a while yet. We went down into town the first day and heard the bad news. I'm surprised it's gotten worse."

Will took notes of how man people lived there. The man told him which close neighbors were gone and which had stayed.

"Thanks a lot. I'm just like a census taker for now."

"We're doing okay. It's not hard to ski down to the Peak 7 lodge if we need help."

Will nodded, closed his logbook and moved on.

. . .

A little neighborhood off Discovery Road of a couple of dozen houses had formed their own little association, sharing food and supplies. They had already raided the unoccupied houses on their street, so there wasn't much for Will to do but list their names and let them know what services were available.

"They've got beef?"

Will nodded. "The county bought the cows from Park County ranchers and they're handing out the meat. But, you've either got to go pick it up at the arena on Boreas Pass road, or to make arrangements to have it delivered on the highway. That's the only plowed road left."

After a discussion, Will promised to deliver their details and request to the city. Their two best skiers planned to cut across country and pick up a bundle of beef at the intersection of the highway and Valley Brook Road. They made a tentative schedule for noon the next day. Will promised that if it fell apart and the delivery couldn't be made, that he would at least get someone to meet the skiers and let them know.

. . .

After a couple of deserted houses, and broken windows to gain access, he was startled by a man wading out into the snow, waving him down.

Will pulled close. "What's the problem?"

"It's my daughter! Can you help?"

Hospital Run

Will helped the man up onto the back seat.

"It's that way," he pointed. Will followed the man's tracks through a narrow path between the trees. A house that had been invisible before came into view.

Will pulled up to the porch. A woman was watching from the door.

"Lily is coughing again," the mother said to her husband.

Will slapped the snow on his suit before he came in. It was a small place, a one-family rental place, probably. The fireplace was lit, and there were mounds of blankets piled on the couch facing it.

The father introduced them, the Severs family. "Lily caught a cold and it's just been getting worse.

The three-year-old coughed and her mother knelt down beside her. "Her fever is worse, I think."

Will handed his laminated sheet to Oscar, the father, and knelt down next to the little girl. He pulled off his glove and said, "Hello, Lily. My name is Will."

She frowned, "Bill?"

"Close. Can I feel your forehead?"

She nodded. The fever was pretty bad. He looked up to the parents. "All the roads are blocked except the highway, and even it is cut off by an avalanche. I can probably carry one adult and Lily and get you to the hospital, but I can't come back for the other one until tomorrow."

Oscar handed the sheet to his wife. "I understand. I know the power is out and I heard that the snow plows stopped, but we're in the dark here. I know we should have left immediately—"

Will shook his head, "Nothing like this has happened in over a hundred and fifty years, never during modern technology. Nobody knew what to do. Don't beat yourself up over it. Let's just get Lily to a doctor."

None of the adults, Will included, knew what to do for Lily other than bundle her up and get her to a hospital.

Oscar said, "June will take her. Let's get her ready."

June was going to have to hold on to stay stable on the back seat of the snowmobile, so she couldn't used her arms to hang on to Lily.

Oscar frowned. "Do we have that papoose thing we used to use when she was little?"

"No, but maybe I can make one." June dug through their clothes and came up with a pair of long-johns. She used the arms and legs to wrap around her neck and behind her back to hold Lily into place against her chest. The little one coughed and cried as she was being forced into the tight quarters.

June sighed. "Oh, no. I can't get my coat over the both of us." The woman was small, five feet or less. Her coat was sized for her frame, and much too small.

Oscar looked frantic. "Use my coat!"

Will looked out the window at the afternoon sky and said, "No, there's a better way." He unzipped his snowmobile suit.

"Mrs. Severs, you wear this. There's enough give to fit you both. Just make sure Lily can breathe. Mr. Severs, I'll wear your coat."

They swapped gear, and Will fastened the unfamiliar jacket. For daytime, it would probably be warm enough.

As soon as Lily realized they were leaving her daddy behind, she started crying. Will nodded. *If she can make that much noise, she's breathing okay.*

Of course, no sooner the thought crossed his mind than she broke into a coughing fit.

"Let's get going," Will said.

"Yes," June agreed.

Oscar reached down to kiss Lily's barely-visible forehead. "You be a good girl and pay attention to Mommy."

Lily was having none of it. She screamed, "Daddy!"

But there was no help for it. Will started up the engine, and barely drowned out the cries. The parents waved and Will pulled away from the house, retracing the path he'd cut getting there.

There was a brief moment when he could actually see the sun, not that he was in any shape to pay attention to sunspots right now. But it was a hopeful sign. Could the day after day of snow be coming to an end?

When the path reached what he knew was Ski Hill Road, he paused. To the right was probably a quicker path. From memory, Ski Hill Road wound through the mountainside and joined Barton Road, which went down to the valley and joined Airport Road. From there he could reach the hospital quicker than retracing his path back to downtown Breckenridge before turning north.

When he paused, June asked, "Is there a problem?"

"No," he yelled back. He turned left.

I can't risk it. Maybe the road that way is quicker if there are no problems. But it's been untouched since the plows stopped. If I get stuck, there's no way she could help me get free. It's too dangerous.

He revved up the engine and raced back along the same path he'd come.

The wind was biting. In spite of the sun, the air here among the trees, surrounded by snow, was like in an icebox. His face and his legs were feeling the brunt of it. He'd trusted the snowmobile suit and without it, his jeans weren't doing a good enough job of keeping his legs protected.

As he passed the better-prepared households, and then the ski lodges, he was tempted to stop, but there was no chance they would be any better prepared to deal with a three-year-old girl with pneumonia than he was. He had to reach the hospital soon.

"How are you doing back there?"

June yelled, "It's cold, but okay."

He could hear Lily's whimpering when the wind was blocked by a tree or a building. *Does she think we're leaving her daddy behind forever? Or does a three-year-old even think that way?*

He raced downslope, easing off the throttle as he entered more congested parts of town.

Park Avenue.

He looked both ways for a snowplow or other traffic. And then eased down onto the road. There was a little snow on the pavement, but he wasn't comfortable driving on the road. It was one of his father's rules, and actually illegal in places.

Still, there was no help for it now.

Around the bend, he could see the sheriff's office. *No stopping now.* He imagined it. Stop and tell the people what was happening. Maybe move June and Lily to a police car. Drive up to the avalanche. Move them back to some snowmobile or snow cat, and then maybe another exchange to a car on the Frisco side of the blockage before they finally were delivered at the hospital.

No. Keep going.

He caught a glimpse of a deputy waiting at the entrance looking at him as he raced by. *I hope they understand.*

Once he turned north onto the highway, he saw evidence of other snowmobile tracks. Only the west side of the road, the southbound lane, was being plowed and cars stayed there, but the northbound lane, now covered maybe three feet deep since they stopped plowing it, was now the semi-official snowmobile lane. He cut across and moved into the tracks of previous snowmobiles.

Another three miles to the avalanche. He cranked the throttle up to full speed.

He had imagined the Swan Mountain avalanche as a huge, oversized snow drift. As he approached, he realized it was something quite different.

Yes, there was a lot of snow there, but it was hardly a smooth drift. There were chunks of ice and whole trees and rocks mixed in like a Godzilla version of almond-chocolate chip ice cream. There was a work crew at the road, filling a dump truck, it looked like.

There was also a police car with its lights flashing. An officer was waving at him with a flashlight.

Will slowed down as he came abreast.

The policeman, not one he knew, looked at the woman and child. "Hospital?"

Will nodded. "As soon as possible."

"Follow the marked route over the avalanche. There's a lot of trees hidden in the snow. Once you make the big turn on the other side, the hospital is on your left. The ER entrance is the one with double-driveways."

"Got it."

The policeman waved him on.

He powered up the marked path, following a snowcat's wide tracks. There were a couple of bends as the route avoided rocks and debris.

From the top, he could see the demolished mobile-home park and the high school beyond. Digging the avalanche out would take a long time. Even if they let it melt in the summer, the debris clearing would be a major undertaking.

We can't blame this on the CME. If you have a heavy snow year, avalanches will happen.

The snowmobile bumped on something and he focused his attention back onto his driving.

Then he was down to the highway. There was a snowmobile path to follow there as well, so he stuck to it. Highway 9 bent slowly to the west, moving away from the ice that covered Dillion Reservoir. Fairly quickly, he saw an entrance to the hospital parking lot.

Double entrance, he said. Shortly, he saw it and pulled in stopping under the overhang at the ER entrance.

There were helping hands easing June and Lily off the seat and assisting her into the entrance. June was explaining Lily's fever.

Will just parked in place and followed them in. He didn't want to lose his snowmobile suit again. And he needed to warm up. His legs were stinging from being blasted by the cold air. Moving around wasn't helping either.

He needn't have worried about losing the Severs. Lily was crying, disturbed out of her cocoon. She saw him. "Bill, where's Daddy? I want Daddy!"

June peeled off the suit and handed it to him. "Thanks for helping us. We didn't know what we were going to do."

The doctor then attracted her attention and Will realized he was just in the way.

He waved to Lily, but that just set her off again.

He carried the suit out of the examination room and one of the attendants asked, "Is that your snowmobile? We need to keep the entrance clear. We can still get ambulances coming in here."

Will sighed. "Sure. Can you give me just a minute? My legs are frozen. I need to get some circulation going."

"Okay, but not long, understand?"

"Yes."

Breckenridge is Buried

He found the beef chunks in the pocket and chewed on a few as he walked in circles in the lobby area.

I wonder if Kelly is here. I really ought to visit her father as well.

But he heard a scream, "I want Daddy!"

Will sighed, glanced at his watch and started pulling the suit on.

Sunset is in an hour. I can do this.

He lashed Oscar's coat into a bundle and strapped it to the snowmobile. He checked the gas and roared out into the parking lot.

Storyteller

Oscar Severs came to the door as Will pulled to a stop.

"What's wrong?"

Will pulled up his goggles. "Nothing other than Lily has been screaming for her daddy the whole time. Do you think you could gather your critical papers and stuff and leave now?"

"Yes! Give me ten minutes."

Will gave him his coat and warned him to layer on more clothes. It was going to be a cold ride. Oscar put out the fire in the fireplace and made sure no candles were left burning. Bundled up and carrying his bag, he got on the back of the snowmobile and Will turned back to race down the road again.

The sun was quickly hidden behind the mountains and even in his snowmobile suit, Will could feel the bite. He knew it was worse for Oscar.

The policeman waved him on when he approached the avalanche. They must have had some idea of what was going on.

Will made sure Lily and her daddy were reunited, and then headed back to Breckenridge at a slower pace.

Sheriff Thompson was waiting for him when he pulled up at the office. It was already dark and the man illuminated the path with his flashlight as Will came in.

"Sorry I'm late. Something came up."

"I gathered. A hospital run—two of them."

"Well it was just one family. The three-year-old was sick." Will gave him the details and turned over the logbook.

Thompson frowned as he looked over the details about the Discovery neighborhood group. "It's late to make an order for food to be delivered, but I guess I'll pull some strings to get it done. The guys over at the arena like to have some warning."

Will nodded. "I told them I couldn't guarantee delivery, but these people are running short on food."

Thompson sighed. "So is everyone. But you did the right thing. We offered help and they asked. I'll have someone there at noon to meet them."

He crooked his fingers and led Will into another office. He flipped a switch and a little desktop printer came on and went through its startup sequence.

"We've got a little power, but none to waste." He put Will's logbook face down on the scanner glass and made a copy, repeating for all the pages he'd filled.

"There. That's it." He handed the logbook back to Will and then turned off the battery-backup box. "Are you still on-board to continue tomorrow?"

Will smiled. "Yes. After I go home and warm up a bit."

"Yes, don't risk your health. The hospital is overloaded as it is."

"I saw."

. . .

His father was waiting for him at the front entrance. He patted his son's back helping him shake off the snow, but Bob put his finger to his lips. He whispered, "Storyteller."

They went in, not attracting too much attention. An old man with a big Santa Claus beard was sitting by the fireplace, sipping a mug.

"Como was the nearest civilization, eighteen miles from where we sit over Boreas Pass." He pointed to the southeast. "There was a rail depot there, on the narrow-gauge railroad, you can still see the old round house. When the Big Snow blocked the rails to Breckenridge, that was where any rescue was likely to come from."

Will unzipped his suit and settled in a chair in range of the fireplace. His mother brought him a bowl of stew. He knew he was late and he was grateful she had saved him some.

He sipped as he listened to the story. He'd heard most of it before—the story of Jess Oakley's cross-country ski to Como get the mail, and the $12 he collected for the run, which was real money back then.

And then there was the sad story of Loren Waldo who lost his way over the pass trying to visit his sick wife in Como and when the body was discovered during the thaw, it was only fifty yards from safety.

Most of the people here were tourists and had never heard the full story of the Big Snow of 1898-9.

Will was struck by a few facts that he'd read before, but forgotten. The first day of the Big Snow brought in five feet of new snow, and by the time it was all done, there had been thirty-two and a half feet of snow, with drifts fifty feet tall in places.

I keep thinking our snow is a rival to the Big Snow, but it's not. It's just a significant snow year, with complications.

He liked the storyteller. He'd missed the introduction, but the guy knew how to hold an audience.

I have stories to tell, but I'm not going to go sit by the fire and keep everyone entertained. Besides, I don't want to look like I'm bragging.

He wondered. Who would really understand what he was doing?

Kelly probably would. My folks, maybe. But he wasn't doing this to tell stories. He just didn't want to be the guy that other people had to take care of. He wanted to be out there doing things.

When the storyteller ended his telling and promised to come by again sometime with new tales, Will got up with the other people as some left to go to bed and others re-arranged the chairs and tables for conversation and games.

He noticed Rick sitting down at a table where some people were going to play Monopoly. The guy seemed to have a perpetual frown.

I guess phone games have their limits.

Will felt a wave of fatigue. If he was going to get out early, then he needed to get some rest as well.

His father was working on some papers in his office. Will chuckled.

"That lamp looks like something out of a Bible story."

Bob nodded. "Same technology probably. The cooks have rendered some of the beef fat into oil. Stick a tuft of cotton into a shallow bowl to use as a wick, and it'll work as a lamp for a while. I'd prefer a candle, but I'll take what I can get."

He looked at his son. "How did your day go?"

Will gave him a summary.

Bob shook his head. "I thought something might have happened, when you got home so late. But I guess a rescue comes first. Same thing again tomorrow?"

"Yes, it's hard to tell from the map, but I think I've only covered a third of the houses in that section. Dad, it's something I can do and I'm glad I've got the opportunity."

He nodded. "There's a new can of gas for you at the bottom of the stairs. I didn't feel like hauling it up. I was pretty tired when I siphoned it."

"Thanks. I know I'll need it."

...

Will started for his bed, but instead went to the west stairwell and went up to the second floor. He went to the Winslow's unit and knocked.

He didn't know whether Kelly was back from visiting her father or not. But if anyone knew, it was probably Beth.

I'm not going in, no matter what. Just talking at the door. That'll be okay, right?

The door opened and some guy in his twenties glared at him.

"Yes, what is it?"

Will put on his employee face. "Oh, sorry to bother you. I was just checking to see if Kelly Winslow had returned from visiting her father."

The man looked puzzled. From inside, Beth called out. "Kyle, Kelly is my roommate. Tell him that no, she hasn't returned yet."

Will nodded. "I heard her. That's all I was interested in. Thank you."

Kyle shrugged and closed the door.

Hmm. Beth is looking for a new guy, it appears. I wonder if Kelly knows about that.

It really wasn't his business, although he would worry if Kelly was home, and had to work around Beth's friends.

Snow catastrophe or not, I guess life goes on.

124

Just because the door was handy, he walked out on the second-floor deck. There wasn't much snow collected since he'd last shoveled it clear.

Is the endless snow finally coming to an end?

He walked over to north edge so he could look out over the streets. There were several ski tracks. Kelly wasn't the only person out and about on skis. But his idle hope that he could see her skiing up was a waste of time. Even with the moonlight filtering through the thin clouds, it was dark. He might have more luck hearing her than seeing her.

She'll turn up eventually. But I need to get some sleep.

Checking the Houses

He peered at his watch and realized he had overslept. Maybe not by much, but Will wanted to stay on his job just like the guys on the work crews. They were going to be gone by the time he tried to beg a lunch.

But Mrs. Kirk had bag for him.

"Thanks. You're a lifesaver."

She smiled. "It sounds like that's your job."

He didn't know quite how to respond to that. Had the story about Lily gotten out? He just nodded and hurried on to go get the gas can and bring the gauge up to over half-full.

Packed and ready. He looked over his map and headed out, turning up Ski Hill Road again.

Even though he was getting a late start, he was still hitting the mountain earlier than the day before. Pulling out of the driveway was a *lot* easier than digging out the shed.

A quarter mile up the road, Kelly was waving her poles.

He pulled to a stop.

"Hi. Fancy meeting you here."

She edged closer. "I'm so glad I caught you. I was going to go up to Peak 8 and if I didn't meet up with you, head back down to the lodge."

"Did you ski here from the hospital?"

She grinned. "Up before dawn, but I made it. And I started from the high school. I was hoping I could tag along today. Is that a problem?"

"No, no problem at all. But how did you know I'd be here."

She leaned up to the back seat and unhooked her skis and pulled the skins off the bottoms. "Oh, there was a little girl, and she told me about Bill."

Will chuckled. "So you met Lily."

"Yes, in spite of the pneumonia, she has a pair of lungs on her."

"So, she did have pneumonia. I was worried we'd panicked for no reason."

Kelly nodded, a little sadly. "There's a lot of that going around. Anyway I talked to her parents and it was plain that 'Bill' was 'Will' and that you're working Ski Hill Road."

She shrugged. "And if I was wrong, I'd still get a good ski day in."

Will helped her strap her skis in place and she settled in on the back seat. "If I have to run someone to the hospital again, I may have to dump you."

She giggled. "That's fine. I can handle myself on the skis."

He knew she could; he just worried a little that bringing her along would get in the way of the job. Not that he'd turn down her offer to keep him company.

With her arms around his waist, he started the engine and moved on.

...

As they moved down the road, he'd occasionally point out a house and tell her about the people or what he found there.

"So you're actually breaking in?"

"That's what they told me to do. I'll break a small window and crawl in. After I do the inventory and leave a note and an IOU for the damage, I'll block the window with a board or tape it with cardboard if I can. I hate that part of the job."

He pulled up when a man waved at him.

"Back again, I see." The man glanced at Kelly but said nothing.

"Yes. More houses to check. Can you pass the word that there should definitely be someone down at the highway at noon to meet your people? The last minute order caused some griping, but the sheriff said he'd pull some strings."

"Great. It's getting a little thin here. We had a deer to share three days ago, but we have a lot of mouths to feed."

Will nodded. "That's the story I hear everywhere."

As they moved on, winding to the side the road to duck under power lines, Kelly patted his shoulder. He slowed down so he could hear her.

"What is it?"

"Are we going to make it? I mean, all of us?"

Will stopped and killed the engine. "How bad is it back on the other side of the avalanche?"

She shook her head slightly. "The people at the hospital are being fed, but not the visitors and family members. At the school, they're doing one meal a day, and it's pretty basic stuff. There are a lot of jokes about finally losing some weight. I haven't heard about anything like the beef handout on the Frisco side.

"People are digging out the pantries for anything that's edible. Of course, I'm not in the know like you are. Maybe the police down there have a plan, but the only thing I heard was strong warnings against looting.

"Which is why I was surprised you were breaking into houses. It sounds like looting."

Will nodded. "I don't like it either. But I've got a paper from the sheriff that says I can, so I have to hope that's enough. Starvation is no joke. We'll all be having stone soup with pine needle tea before long unless the city can find more food somewhere.

"And that's why I have to inventory these houses. A few hidden bags of flour in an idle pantry could save lives."

Kelly nodded. "I understand. It's just like the Big Snow I heard of, right. The town had to survive months with no shipments from the outside."

"Yeah, but there's a difference. What was the population of Breckenridge back in 1898? And what's the population now, during ski season no less, with all the hotels and condos full? It's not like we can send out hunters to shoot a few deer to tide us through.

"Back then, there were no snowplows and people had sleds and horses to pull them. People planned for the snow better in those times. Not like us. We think it's the end of the world when the snowplow is a little bit late. Usually modern life goes on and if you're hungry, all you do is go to the nearest restaurant."

He shook his head. "We weren't prepared for this. How could we have been? In another hundred and fifty years, if this happens again, those people won't be prepared either.

"Every day, I hope to hear about another shipment of beef from over the pass. Eating the same thing every day might get old, but it's better than drinking warm water just to keep your stomach full."

She shivered. "I want this to be over."

"I've been meaning to ask. How is your father?"

"Oh, so-so. They've got his leg in a cast, but he has double-pneumonia and they're worried about that."

She frowned. "Could you hold off starting the engine for a minute?"

"Okay."

She pulled out her little blue radio and pushed the button a couple of times.

"Daddy, are you listening?"

"Kelly? Did you make it back safely?" The man's voice was clear, but weak, and he coughed.

"Yes, I'm fine. Safe and sound. I just wanted to check up on you."

"Bored as usual. Roger wants to play poker some more, but I'm not sure he doesn't cheat."

In the background another voice shouted, "Hey!"

Kelly laughed. "Just don't lose any of my college fund, okay?"

Her father coughed and said, "No. That's as safe as it's always been."

"Okay, Daddy. I've got to go now. Just checking on you."

"Bye. Be safe."

Kelly put her radio in her pocket. "That was a joke," she explained. "I don't have any college fund. A few years ago, he apologized and said he'd never have enough money to send me to college. Since then, I'm always joking about him spending my college fund."

Will nodded. "Olympic athletes don't make much money?"

She laughed. "Nope. Not unless you're famous and can make a big endorsement deal from a big-name sports company. There are prizes from some international competitions, and such. But many, like Daddy, have to rely on a sponsor."

"Who's his sponsor?"

Kelly shook her head. "Later. Your job is important. I shouldn't be wasting your time."

He got the message and nodded as if it was no big deal and started the engine.

...

The first two houses they stopped at were occupied and Will explained what the city was doing. They hadn't heard about the avalanche and Kelly waved her hands as she explained what she had seen.

Then, there was a whole side-street that was vacated, as if they'd all gotten together and agreed to clear out that first day. Two of the houses had left a door unlocked—on one house it was the main entrance, and on another there was a side entrance. The other houses had windows that had to be subjected to the ball-peen hammer that Will had brought along.

Kelly was a big help surveying the houses. Will was filling pages with all the resources they found.

"Wow. This propane tank is full. I bet your Mom would like that. She was griping about how hard it was cooking over the wood fires."

Will nodded, "Yeah, but all we do is write it down. The instant I carry something home for the lodge to use, then it's looting. I'm sure the city will send a snowcat up to gather the most needed things we find, but that's not my decision to make."

He taped a double-layer of cardboard over the broken window and they left by the front door. He couldn't use the dead-bolt that way, but it had been a tight fit crawling through that window as it was.

...

An hour later, they came across three men who had felled a large tree. Will made his introductions.

"That's good to know," said one of the men. "But right now all I'm concerned with it getting this firewood back to the house before dark. We should have cut a smaller tree."

One of the others said, "Yeah, but we agreed to concentrate on the dead ones. We were going to have to get rid of all these pine-beetle trees eventually."

Will asked, "Are you going to cut it up?"

"I guess. None of us are experienced at this. We tried to drag it, but it's too big."

"Got a chain or a rope? I could try to help."

They had a rope and Will fastened it to the frame of the snowmobile. He was a little worried that he might bend something, but it was worth a try.

He pulled and the snowmobile threw the white stuff high as he dug in, but at first it didn't budge.

The men grabbed hold and added their strength, rocking the tree, and then it began to move.

Following yelled instructions, Will pulled it the two hundred yards to their house. The men, with profuse thanks, turned to the task of chopping the tree into firewood. Will made some notes on his log and moved on.

. . .

Kelly laughed. "That was fun. More satisfying than ransacking someone's house."

"Yeah. But who knows what—"

A rifle shot echoed through the trees and a small spray of snow showed where the bullet had hit.

"I shoot all looters!" the voice yelled from a distance.

Will pushed Kelly down low, hunting for any sign of the shooter. "We're not looters! I'm working with the sheriff!"

"Stay clear of my place, or I'll shoot!"

Warmth

Will could tell the direction, at least, so he revved the engine and turned back to the main road.

Out of range, he stopped. "Are you okay?"

Her teeth chattered. "Scared to death, but okay."

He pulled out his log book and map and tried to identify the location of the shooter. "I don't think I'll be checking *those* houses."

He frowned at the map. "I wish I could tell what range that guy considers his territory. I've still got to check a lot of houses around here."

She laughed nervously. "You're still on the job. I'd be skiing like mad for home."

He looked up at the sky. "I can't leave yet. I've still got a couple of hours of daylight before I need to turn back." He looked at her. "I will take you home, though, if that's what you want."

She hesitated. "You tempt me. But, if you think we can stay clear of that maniac, then okay. Are you going to tell the police?"

"Yes, of course, but don't expect them to come out here and arrest him."

"Why not? He's shooting at people."

"I'm not happy about it either, but it was just a warning shot. Something to get our attention. I'm sure he could make the argument that he wasn't shooting at anyone.

"The police are so hard up for manpower that they are using guys like me to do their job. Yes, I'll warn them, but just so they'll have a bullhorn handy when they follow up with a snowcat."

Kelly grumbled. "There's no excuse for shooting at people."

"Real looters are a life-and-death problem for people surviving on the edge out here, and the police aren't where you can call them for help."

"I'm just saying." She sniffed.

. . .

He pulled up beside the two-story house, obviously unoccupied. "Interesting."

"What's interesting?" Kelly asked.

"Well, for one thing, that snowdrift on the side goes all the way up to that balcony. And for another, there are icicles hanging from the roof."

"Oh-kay...." She looked at him for more information.

"I'm going to check the door first. We might be lucky."

He slipped on his snowshoes and walked up to the porch. Half of it was covered by the drift, but not the door. He checked it. "It's locked."

He walked back a bit and then chose a easy slope up to the top of the drift.

"What are you doing?" Kelly asked.

He stretched out his arm and grabbed the railing on the balcony. "Well, one thing I've noticed at the lodge is that on the ground floor, people lock their windows, but on the upper floors, they don't."

It was difficult wearing snowshoes, but he hooked one leg over the balcony and climbed onto the boards. He checked the sliding glass door and after shaking it, it opened. "Like I hoped. I'll open the front door for you."

A couple of minutes later, he worked the latches and the door opened. She walked in. "Whoa!"

"Right! Those icicles gave it away. The last people here left the heater running. I suppose they wanted to keep the pipes from freezing, but it's in the seventies—way too hot."

Kelly nodded and unzipped her jacket and peeled it off her shoulders. She sagged onto the warm couch. "This is nice."

Will found the thermostat and turned it down to its lowest setting. "It's not going to save the pipes if they burn all their propane in the first few days." He glanced over at the girl, stretched out on the couch.

Far too tempting a picture. But he did unzip his suit as well, tying the sleeves around his waist.

"I'll start the inventory."

She smiled. "Oh, I'll help. It's just that you don't get this luxury these days."

"It's even warmer upstairs." *Where the beds are.*

He concentrated on work, not that he didn't smile her way frequently. The propane was down to 20%, but the pantry was full and the spice cabinet would make his mother drool. He wrote it all down.

When he found a piece of paper to write his note to the property owners, he mentioned it all, including how he got in and the change he'd made to the heater.

Kelly patted the couch beside her. "Come sit for a minute."

He didn't turn down the offer.

"How are you holding up?" Will asked.

"Great! Really. In spite of that thing that got my heart racing. Now don't take this the wrong way, but...."

"But?"

She quickly kissed him on the cheek. "Sorry, but I've been keyed up. That's not an invitation to do it again."

"Oh? Warn me next time so I can get my lips properly aligned."

She chuckled. She patted his hand. "We'd better get moving."

He sighed. "You're right. Zip up. It's cold outside."

...

She patted him on the shoulder as he passed the Peak 8 lodge on their way back. It had gotten dark. He slowed to a stop and killed the engine.

"I'm getting off here. I'll cut over and take the 4 O'Clock Run down."

Will nodded. "I've got to go to the sheriff's office and report in."

She climbed off the snowmobile and collected her skis.

"Tell them about the shooter."

"I will. Don't worry. Oh! I totally forgot!"

"What's that?"

"Um. You might want to knock on your door before barging in. When I went by your room to check on you last night, there was a guy there—Kyle somebody. He was with Beth, and he really didn't like the idea that some guy was knocking on the door."

Kelly grinned. "Well, I'm not surprised. I should have guessed something like that would happen."

"Oh?"

"Yeah. Beth and I talked a lot. I got to know her a bit, and she's one of those girls who really *needs* a guy in her life. We even talked about what would happen when Dad comes back from the hospital. She said that she'd probably have a new guy to move in with by then. I didn't realize she was working at it so quickly. Thanks for the warning."

Will watched her affix her skis and push away. He was glad she had some moonlight.

He started the engine and moved off slowly. She took a branch to the right before too long, cutting through some street to get to the ski trail.

...

Thompson nodded as he read and copied Will's notes. "Sorry you got shot at. And I think you're right, it was probably just a warning. I'll make some notes on this to deal with later. You stay clear of the guy. You don't have the uniform and you don't have a badge."

Will chuckled. "I'm not planning to get anywhere close to him." None of his notes had mentioned Kelly and he wasn't about to mention her either. "Tomorrow's route won't go past his place."

Thompson said, "Oh, by the way. We got a food delivery truck over the pass this afternoon. A small truck, but every bit helps."

"Variety. That's nice."

...

Will took his time returning to the lodge. He suspected Kelly was already there, but he didn't want any chance of them arriving at the same time and prompting uncomfortable questions. He took the Main Street route, although there was no street to speak of.

I've got to be careful in town. I don't want to collapse anyone's tunnel.

But he moved cautiously, cutting back to Park when he reached Watson Avenue. But something was wrong. He couldn't put a finger on it. It annoyed him so much that he killed the engine and just listened in the dark.

And then he realized. It was really dark, and the headlights had masked that.

He looked up. There was no moon. Heavy dark clouds were moving into the valley.

Will sighed. "So much for sunlight tomorrow."

Rick's Problem

He was in time for supper. Hurriedly, he went to his room and shed the suit and put on his light jacket instead. He saw Kelly eating with Beth and Kyle. He nodded and Kelly made eye contact with a smile, but made no effort to invite him to their group.

His mother filled his bowl. "Did you have a nice day?"

"It was busy. I think the highlight was when I found a house that had left their gas heater on. I haven't felt so warm in ages."

She shook her head. "Did you fix it?"

He nodded. "Still, you don't know how nice little things are until they're gone."

He wasn't about to tell his parents about the warning shot. That was a quick way to get his permission to ride out on the snowmobile revoked.

As he looked around for a place to sit, he realized just how well he was getting to know these people. Usually, guests came for a weekend and left. He might get to know their last name, but only because it was on the paperwork.

But as he found a place against the wall to sit, he realized he could name maybe half the people, as well as know which family group they were in.

Just out of hearing range, Rick Torino was arguing with his older sister Julia. Rick had a stubborn look on is face and Julia's gestures indicated that she wasn't going to help. If he could read lips, she might be saying, "There's no help for it."

Over at a table near the fireplace, Mr. and Mrs. Torino were with their little daughter Teresa. The mother had her eyes on her oldest children, too. Will wondered how much she could read their body language.

Probably better at it than I am.

He ate his stew. It was getting a little thinner every day. They must not have received more food from the city yet. But he shouldn't gripe. Getting a lunch as a worker meant he was eating better than the rest of them.

I wonder how soon the city will go collect the food I've identified.

. . .

Rick sat down beside him. Will could see that same angry expression on his face.

"What's up? Run out of games to play?"

Rick didn't look up from his hands. "No." He glanced over at his family.

"Will, you've got a snowmobile, don't ya? Is there any chance you could take me back to my place?"

"What's the problem? Wasn't your place demolished?"

"Yeah, but...."

Will frowned. "Is there something you want to salvage?"

Rick hesitated, then nodded. "Yes. Something I need."

Will had a horrible suspicion that Rick had a drug stash. But that didn't seem right. *He doesn't have the shakes, and I've never seen that kind of look in his eyes.*

"Rick, it's been days, and the snow keeps coming down. Anything you left is going to be buried in the snow. If it's perishable, or suffers water damage, then sorry, it's a lost cause. If not, you may just have to wait for summer for everything to thaw out."

Rick shook his head. "That's not good enough. It'll be too late."

Will said, "Come with me." He got up and walked his bowl over to the kitchen. He gestured and they went to the stairs.

When they walked out onto the second-floor deck, the snow was coming down hard. Will buttoned up his collar.

"The same snow is coming down on your place. I'm surprised the mobile homes weren't buried before the avalanche came. There's no chance you'll be able to dig in the rubble."

He turned to face Rick, in a lighter jacket than his, shivering in the cold. "What is it you're looking for?"

The kid sighed. He looked back to make sure no one was listening. "You can't tell anyone."

Will chuckled. "Anything short of a hidden meth lab."

Rick shook his head. "Nothing like that." He took a deep breath. "It's not a thing. It's a person."

"Oh? Who?"

"Mary Patterson."

"Doug's little sister?"

Rick nodded. "She lives in the same mobile home park, but I don't think their place was hit. We've, ah .... We've sorta been dating, but no one knows."

Rick was sixteen, only two years younger than he was, but Will had been thinking of him as a little kid.

I'd have been dating at his age if I'd ever had the chance.

"Come on back inside."

They brushed the snow off as well as they could.

"I can't take you there, not for days at least. I've got a job for the sheriff that takes priority. But ... every now and then I go close to your place, taking people to the hospital over the avalanche.

"If you want, I can take a message, or maybe ask if the Pattersons are still there at the mobile home park. I know the police keep track of people like your family that have had to be relocated."

Rick frowned. "But no one can know that it's me looking for Mary. Hmm. Can you take a letter?"

"It might be hard to get it to her secretly, but I can carry it. I'm not the post office. I can't guarantee it'll get to her."

Rick nodded eagerly. "That's great. I have to do something!"

...

Out of habit, Will grabbed a shovel after Rick left and shoveled a path from the west side to the east. *Why am I doing this? It'll all be covered by morning anyway.*

He couldn't help but compare Rick's desperation to his own timidity. Just how intense were Rick and Mary? Other than that one kiss and the occasional gloved hand-in-hand, his relationship with Kelly was more companionship than physical.

But just give me a chance. I could be as brave as Rick.

Frustrated, he went down to the front entrance to check on the snow-mobile. It would be rough going, making headway through a fresh base of powder. He shoveled the front driveway under the canopy.

His shovel bumped up against the gas can hidden under the snow. It sounded empty.

He lifted it. *Yes, I'd better take care of this.* He went down to the garage and found the siphon hose in the storage room. There was a pad of paper, on the first few sheets, his father had written, "Five gallons was siphoned from your gas tank. Please check with the front desk before you leave."

Will nodded. *Dad's version of an IOU.*

With the flashlight in hand, he walked down the aisle, looking for a car to tap.

The problem was that most cars had locks on their gas-cap doors. He saw his father's note under the windshield wiper on a couple of cars.

There! He saw a Jeep with a bare gas cap lid. He fished the hose into the tank and the other end into the jerrycan. He squeezed the bulb on the hose until the gas started flowing. He watched to make sure it wouldn't overflow, but the gas dribbled to a stop before he finished.

Oops! I must have drained the tank. Oh well, it's enough. I don't use that much gas during a day anyway. Their snowmobile did over a hundred and fifty miles on a full tank, and he wasn't going anywhere near that distance.

He put the notice on the Jeep's windshield and put the hose back in the storeroom.

At least the gas can was slightly easier to carry up the stairs. He emptied it into the snowmobile's tank. The wind was howling and the snow was swirling down, even under the canopy. *Ready to go in the morning.*

There was a tug on his sleeve.

Will turned and saw Kelly right behind him.

"You're not dressed for outside. I didn't even hear you coming through the door."

She nodded, shivering. "I waited until no one was looking and crept through. I had to talk to you. Is it okay if I come along with you tomorrow?"

He nodded toward the snow. "It's coming down hard. Likely to be colder tomorrow."

She sniffed at the weather. "I've been out in this stuff since I was a toddler."

He put his hand on her shoulder. "You're shivering."

"Only because I'm not dressed right. But, can I come?"

He nodded. "If they don't catch you."

"I'll meet you up on the hill, like yesterday."

"They'll see you at the entrance, especially with your skis."

She grinned. "If you push hard, you can still make it out the north entrance. In another couple of days, at this rate, I'll be able to ski off the deck."

He chuckled. "You just might at that."

Relapse

Will was up early. He dressed quietly, and almost bumped into his mother, also dressing early to help with the breakfast preparations.

"Did your watch wake you up early?" she asked.

"No, I just have some things to do before I can leave. There was a lot of snow last night."

She nodded, and sighed. "I worry about you going out there. When you were late that day, I was sure you were stranded in the snow somewhere."

"No, Mom. I'm in and out of houses all day long. Even if I get stranded, I'll be safe."

She shook her head, not really convinced.

He patted her on the back, suddenly aware that he was taller than she was. "I'll be fine."

He hurried to the first floor deck and peered around at the north entrance on the west side. The ground looked undisturbed, but even with two feet of fresh snow, it was clear that *someone* had been using that entrance fairly recently. The snow was scraped in an arc by the door itself—much higher beyond that little circle.

He was tempted to go clear the platform there at the top of the steps, but that would put the both of them together and just make it all the more likely that she'd be discovered.

He shoveled on the deck quietly as possible, and Kelly was right, the place where he'd been dumping snow off the edge had built up a huge pile almost as tall as the deck itself. With the fresh snow on top of it, someone could climb over the edge and ski all the way down to Ski Hill Road.

There was a little scrape. He could barely hear it, but he looked over at the entrance and she was shoving at the door, wedging the fresh powder out of the way with brute force.

But Kelly was small, she didn't have to open the door all the way. She crawled through the gap and carried her skis and poles through before pushing it closed.

Will could have spoken and attracted her attention, but she was plainly *sneaking,* silently making her escape. He didn't want to startle her.

She put on her skis at the top of the landing and skied down the stairs, or rather the snowy ramp that covered the stairs. She zipped away and was off on the road before he could do anything more.

Good. She's away. Now I've got to get moving.

He picked up a small bag of dumplings for his lunch and hurried to the front entrance.

There was a white envelope wedged in the windshield of the snowmobile.

He brushed the snow off of it. It was sealed, addressed only to Mary Patterson.

Will slid it into an inside pocket of his suit and started up the engine.

I wonder what Rick wrote? Is it a love letter? A plan for them to get together?

He wasn't about to pry the edges and sneak a peek. It would be embarrassing, no matter what. But it was also plain that he had to hand it to Mary personally. Parents were known to peek at their children's correspondence.

. . .

Kelly waved and he picked her up.

She shook her head. "It's harder to ski uphill today. I was just going to find a place to stop and wait for you. You're out earlier today."

"I got up early to watch you sneak out the north entrance. It was a tight squeeze."

She sat on the back seat and put her arms around him. "You should have said something."

"More fun to watch."

With two feet of fresh snow, the roads looked like they'd never been touched. They'd even beaten the snowcat out so they had the world to themselves.

Kelly said, "You *do* know which way to go, right?"

"I think I've got this map memorized. Good thing I don't have to rely on my phone's GPS."

"Is it out?"

"I don't really know. There's a location dot, but I can't load the background maps, since the internet is dead. So it's just a lone dot on a blank grid. Useless."

"Dad had a map program that downloaded all the maps so it would work out of range of the towers, but I don't think he's used it in years."

"Yeah, I knew about a couple of navigation apps like that, but … you don't think about it before the sun goes burp. Of course, the CME might have taken out the GPS satellites too, so you never know."

...

They'd made contact with two families and had inventoried four vacant houses when Kelly's radio started making noise.

Will killed the engine.

Kelly worriedly held up the blue radio to her head, pushing the cap off her ear.

"Daddy, is that you?"

It was a woman's voice. "Hello? Is this Kelly Winslow? Sam Winslow's daughter?"

"Yes! Is Daddy okay?"

"Well, his fever has spiked and he's a little delirious. The man in the next bed said you were a cross-country skier and could be contacted on this radio. So … I just thought you should know."

"Yes, of course! I'll get there as soon as I can."

"I don't think he's in real danger, so if it's too bad out, don't risk it."

"I *will* be there. Don't worry."

Will waited until she put her radio away. "I can get you there faster." He pulled out his map. "If we go ahead, it's closer this way, but I've never taken this road before. There's a risk it might be impassable."

Kelly could ski faster than him driving snowmobile downhill but most of the trip to the hospital was on relatively flat land at the base of the valley. But more than that, the story of Loren Waldo crept into his head, lost in the snow trying to see his sick wife.

He needed to get Kelly safely to the hospital, especially in today's weather.

"I'd appreciate the ride," she nodded. "And the quicker the better. The road north will probably be okay."

Will double-checked the cords holding Kelly's skis and poles in place. The ride might get rough.

"Hang on tight." She did.

The untraveled roads weren't totally pristine. Something big and four-legged had plowed across the road at one point. Will didn't *think* there were moose on the mountain, but he knew they were in range. Had one of them been forced out of its home by the snow?

You need to be careful. This area is filled with hungry people with guns.

But he didn't have time to stop and look at the prints to see if it was a moose or just a big deer or an elk.

He really didn't want to come to a stop for any reason. He didn't want to lose the momentum plowing through the deep unpacked snow. He could probably dig them out if he got buried, but all that would take time.

There were more houses he'd have to visit before he was done with this section. He barely glanced at them as he passed by.

He was glad Kelly had wanted to come along. It made the task a lot more fun. But if she had to be by her father, then he totally understood.

His own family always seemed a pain, but he'd be lost without them.

Sooner than he expected, the road opened up on a collection of larger buildings.

"Airport Road!" He yelled over the engine noise.

There were signs that Airport had been plowed and traveled in the last few days. The road was on a cliff overlooking the buildings. The area below had been graded flat a long time ago. It was an easy choice to turn left and follow the road rather than risk going down the slope and try to cut through the buildings.

Another bend, and the road joined the highway. They'd made it through the unknown route, and saved time doing it. He smiled.

Off in the distance, he saw some men working. He couldn't tell what they were doing at first.

Kelly yelled. "Sweeping the solar panels!" She must have been reading his mind.

He could see it then. Local solar power was going to be critical if the power grid was down the one to two years that Lloyds document projected for the most remote areas. But to use it, they had to keep the solar panels from being buried in the snow.

Maybe a mile later on the right, he saw several smoke columns off to the right. He nodded. The Tiger Run RV park. How many of those were stranded? Certainly an RV was more hard up for gasoline than a car. *Probably they have a neighborhood association now, just like everyone else.* Groups had to band together to make it through.

He was almost on top of the avalanche before the swirling snow cleared enough to reveal the temporary white hill that had blocked off the valley. He got a quick glimpse of the work crew before he had to cut to the side and take the snowmobile path.

The clearing operation looked more organized than the last time he'd seen it. In addition to the men with shovels, there was a Bobcat, using it's power shovel to lift snow and debris too heavy to handle manually. There was also a dump truck that it was filling with snow.

But Will had to concentrate on the path over. The recent snow had altered the look of the trail.

Then quickly, he was over and pulled into the hospital parking lot. He pulled up to the ER entrance.

"Just go. I'll bring your skis after I park."

She nodded and hurried into the entrance.

Will unstrapped her gear and walked it into the hospital. He asked at the desk, "Where can I store this for Kelly Winslow?"

They gave him a tag to affix to the bundle and had him set them next to the entrance.

I'd better let her know where they are.

Rick's Note

There was a big whiteboard that listed patients and locations. He saw Sam Winslow's name and not far down, he noticed Lily Severs.

I can't waste much time, but I can look in the door.

Lily's room was closer, he peeked in and saw four beds and five small children in what looked like a private, one-person room. There were a couple of mothers dozing in chairs against the wall.

Lily shouted, "Bill!" She held out her arms.

"Hello, Lily." He glanced at the ladies. One of them looked like a very tired June Severs. She nodded permission.

Will picked Lily up from the mattress and held her. "How are you doing?"

Lily coughed at him. "I'm fine! June and Mary let me play with their dolls. Can you play with us?"

Will nodded to the other two little girls. "No, I'm sorry, I just dropped by to see how you were."

"I'm fine!" She had the words down.

Will set her back down and whispered to her mother. "How are you doing here?"

June shrugged. "It's tough. Oscar and I get to share a cot over at the school—although not at the same time," she grinned. "The Frisco Recovery Group say we can move to a shelter with a real bed as soon as the doctors sign off on Lily. Maybe in a day or so."

He nodded. "Interesting times."

She shuddered. "You can say that again. But, thanks for checking up on us."

. . .

Sam Winslow was the second bed in a row of five with barely a foot between them. When Will entered the room, Kelly didn't notice him as she stood at the foot of the bed, chewing her thumb, watching her father breathe. Sam's neighbor to the right nodded at him.

Will put his hand on Kelly's shoulder. "How is he doing?"

She shook her head. "They don't know yet. I'm supposed to be patient."

He sighed. "I left your skis at the place by the entrance. They're marked. I also left my Mom's dumplings for you."

She frowned. "I can't take that."

"Yes, you can. I'll be back at the lodge for supper and they don't feed you here. That's what you said. You'll need the calories. I was going to share them with you anyway."

She hesitated and then nodded. "Okay. Thanks."

Will gave her shoulder a squeeze. "I would stay longer, but...."

She nodded. "Back to work. It's important. I know."

"Don't overtax yourself. Find a chair and rest when you can."

"Go. I've been here before."

"I'm Roger, by the way," said the man in the next bed, also with his leg in a cast. "I'll keep an eye on her."

Will nodded. "Thanks."

. . .

I hate to take the time, but this may be my only opportunity.

He took the snowmobile over to the remnant of the mobile home park.

Only the northern side of the park had remained unburied by the avalanche, maybe a dozen mobile homes and a couple of slightly larger storage buildings. With the streets shoveled to the buildings, the whole place was surrounded by a snow wall. *It looks like a pit dug into the snow.* But he knew it wasn't.

He stopped the snowmobile and walked down the ramp to the fireplace burning in the middle of the street. People nodded.

"Are the Pattersons here?"

"Yeah. Who's asking?"

Will held out his gloved hand. "I'm Will Parker, from River Mountain Lodge. Several of the families that lived here; the Torinos, the Fosters, Ruth Dent and her family and some others are now staying at the lodge. I'd been asked to drop by the next time I was in the neighborhood and see how people were doing."

"Greg Wilson." The man shook his hand. "I'm glad they're somewhere safe. You wanted the Pattersons?"

"Oh, I just know Doug from school. But your neighbors were interested in how you all were holding up."

"I was about to go there anyway. You can help."

Greg went to the big fireplace built out of a metal tank and with a poker fished out two red-hot buckets filled with rocks. He handed Will a thick insulated rag. "Carry it carefully. It'll burn your leg if it bumps up against you."

Will watched how Greg carried his bucket and did the same.

Greg explained as they slowly carried the loads. "Most of the units are out of propane. But we can put a pail of hot rocks in the oven and it'll keep the place mostly warm."

Will nodded. "We've got the same problem at the lodge. Maybe I'll try this back there."

Greg knocked on the door.

Doug answered. "Yeah?"

"Friend come visiting." Greg moved on to the next mobile home.

Doug smiled when he opened the door. "Will! What're you doing here?"

"It looks like I'm delivering hot rocks."

Doug laughed. "Great. Wait 'til I empty out the oven."

Shortly the old rocks were sitting out in the snow and the open oven door was radiating heat into the kitchen.

Mary Patterson was bundled up like she was on the ski slope, but she offered Will a cup of tea. "I'll just have to warm the water now that we've got fresh heat."

"Oh, I can't stay long. I'm just checking on you for your neighbors, like the Fosters and the Torinos."

Will chatted about how people were doing at the lodge. Doug said, "I can make you a list of how many people are still here."

"That would be great. The police have a list of the people who've been relocated, but if I can let them know how you're doing, it'd relieve some worries."

As Doug hurried out to ask a couple of questions from his neighbors, Mary told Will how their father was out helping with the avalanche clearance crew.

Will nodded and slipped the envelope from his pocket and handed it to her.

She said nothing, asking no questions, and quickly made it vanish.

Doug came back with his answers and finished his list for Will.

"That'll be great. But now I've got to go back to my task." He gave them a short version of his job and how it was playing out.

With an invitation to come back and visit again, Will finally insisted he had to get back to his job and pulled away from the little community, still struggling to make do in spite of the number who died in the avalanche and their missing neighbors.

Mary didn't bat an eye when I showed her the letter. It was like she had expected it. He grinned. Probably she and Rick had been keeping secrets for a while.

But before he'd gotten up to speed, he saw a bus and a utility truck. People were climbing into the bus and others were loading the Bobcat onto the truck. He pulled up close.

"What's going on?"

A man yelled back. "New avalanche. Hoosier Pass is closed. We're going to work there now."

Will nodded and waved before he drove away.

This is bad. Being unable to drive to Frisco, Silverthorne and Dillon is bad, but they're so hard up we weren't getting any supplies from them anyway.

But with Hoosier Pass closed, that means no more cattle from Park County. No more food trucks, and any replacement diesel for the snowplows is out of the picture.

I really hope they can clear it fast.

But that also meant his own job, finding resources in abandoned houses, was even more important than before. His faint impulse to go home early today was gone.

He needed to get back to the Ski Hill Road and get to work! He'd wasted too much time already today.

He revved the engine and headed south at full speed.

Misjudgment

He almost missed Coyle Valley Road, which was the turn to get to Airport Road.

I wish we still had an airport. He looked over to the buildings that had taken the place of the short dirt airstrip from fifty years ago. Someone had told him it was a private strip that had only lasted a few years—just long enough to name the road, he guessed. One of the guests had said that at 9000 feet, small planes would have a hard time landing or taking off here anyway. There were cars parked there now—day-trippers from Denver who had been stranded.

He was following his own track through the snow by the time he started uphill, and he was glad of it. The snow was so loose in places that he skidded backward even with the engine running full speed.

It had taken longer than he'd hoped, but he made it back to the last house that Kelly had helped him with. He checked his log and then moved to the next house.

...

It was plain when he needed to quit. With only daylight through the window to let him explore the next house, Will found himself stumbling in the fading light of evening. He had a flashlight, but no replacement batteries. He was saving that for emergencies.

I could always use my cell phone, I guess. But that battery level was low as well. He couldn't count on it.

And this house has been a bust. I guess it's time to go home.

It was clear the place had been emptied out well before the solar storm. Perhaps the owner had left it idle for the year. There was nothing in the pantry, no propane, and even the water tank had been drained.

He made notes in his log book and went back outside, leaving an empty cardboard box propped up against the broken window, weighed down with a stack of books.

What a waste of a good window for nothing.

He got back on the snowmobile and started it up.

The gas gauge was reading empty. *Uh-oh. I didn't realize it was so low.*

It had been a busy day and he'd started off with less gas than normal. He regretted all the times he'd let the engine idle while checking out a house to see if it was occupied.

Do I have enough gas to make it back to the lodge?

He wasn't really sure. *Maybe....* He looked at his logbook by the light of the headlights and double-checked. Yes. Two houses over he'd seen a two-gallon gasoline can beside a portable generator. It was worth a shot.

Quickly, he drove over to the place and crawled back through the window and found the can he remembered. He lifted it. He gave it a shake. *Nearly nothing. But anything is better than nothing.*

He poured it into his snowmobile, left the empty can on the porch and started home.

Which is quicker? I've just got to trust that I can make it. Take Ski Hill back, or cut down to Airport?

He was closer to Airport and he'd left a trail to follow. He pulled out his map.

Illuminated by the reflection of his headlights on the snow, he could see a possibility. There were two paths between the Breckenridge ski area and his current position. He'd been taking the winding path among the houses, but there was an alternate road, nearly barren of houses that probably ran through national forest land. He'd avoided it before of because the guy with the gun and because he was supposed to be visiting the houses anyway.

But that's actually my easiest route home. I can stay at even throttle and not have to wind through the houses.

He stuffed the map back into his pocket and moved off, taking the turn and making his easy way between the walls of trees on either side of the untracked snow. The headlights showed little sign of deer or other animals since the last snowfall.

Then, the headlights dimmed and the engine stuttered. He played with the throttle, but the snowmobile had a mind of its own. *I can't be running out of gas. I just added some.*

But the engine shuddered to a stop. He turned the key, and although it tried to start once, that was it.

It was clear what had happened. *Stupid. Was that gas I added any good, or did I just run out?*

What could he do now?

He pulled out the flashlight and the map. *How close am I to a house, any house?*

In the dark, with flakes still falling, his highest priority was getting to shelter. Finding more gas was a problem for tomorrow.

Mom is going to worry when I don't show up for supper. But I told her I could easily find shelter. I just have to make it true.

He clicked off the flashlight. It was very dark out, but he couldn't waste his battery on comfort light.

The snowmobile is in the middle of the road, but nothing is going to run into it.

He made sure his suit was zipped up all the way. Then he pulled out his snowshoes. He was going to have to walk to shelter.

Are the nearest houses on the road, or could I save time by cutting through the trees. If I turned left, I know I'd run into some house eventually, if I didn't get lost and start walking in circles.

No. Stick to the road.

I wonder if that guy with the gun lives near here. Surely he's not out walking around after sunset, is he?

Will smiled. *I could always ask for directions if he shows up, I suppose.*

He stepped out into the darkness. It was coming down hard, and with no light. He was startled a couple of minutes later when he almost walked into a tree.

Three seconds from the flashlight showed him the correct path and he walked on.

Walking on snowshoes in thick powder wasn't at all like downtown sidewalks. He stumbled and had to pick himself back up a few times. Snow that worked its way down his collar was unpleasant.

Surely there'll be a turn off into a neighborhood soon!

But the snow seemed endless, and he was using two second bursts of flashlight more often than he liked, just to convince himself that he was still on the road.

It was quiet, but not a silent night. Occasionally, there was crack as some tree branch finally reached its breaking point. The snow came and went, and once, the heavy flakes made a sound of their own, like a faint hiss.

He unzipped his collar a bit, to let off the heat of his exertions. It was freezing out, but no wind.

And then, a blink of the flashlight showed a side road. *But that's on the right. I know all the houses are on the left.*

He fumbled for his map. It was a road over to the ski slopes. Probably if he had skis, it might be tempting to go that way and ski down to the Peak 7 Lodge.

That's ridiculous. Kelly could do it, but not me. And not on my snowshoes.

He took another bearing with his flashlight. Up ahead, there was a glint of reflection. He hurried on faster.

When he reached the light, it turned out to be a tiny rod with a ribbon attached. He wiggled it.

Oh. I'm standing on a car. This is a radio antenna.

He considered it. Just below his feet was a bubble of air surrounded by the insulation of the snow itself. He *could* dig down, open the door somehow, and have shelter for the night.

Yeah, right. I'd end up having to break the window, and do I even have a tool to hit it with? And then, no comforting bubble out of the weather. Ridiculous.

There were houses not too far away. He knew it. All he had to do was find one of them. Break in, wait out the weather until morning, and then find gas somewhere to get the snowmobile running again.

He aimed his feet down the road. Lift. Slog ahead. Repeat.

A house appeared, right off the road. He climbed to the porch and knocked.

There was no response. *That's okay, there was only a fifty-fifty chance anyway.* He tried the door, but it was locked. Peering closely with his flashlight showed the deadbolt in place.

So it was the window. He moved over, and sagged down on his knees. There were burglar bars securing the place. He wasn't going to get in this one.

He tried to remember if he'd visited it before, but he didn't think so. This was probably one he'd skipped because it was too close to the shooter.

Just move on. I'm really getting tired. And he was getting a headache as well. How long had he been hiking?

He stared at his wristwatch dumbly for a moment, before he used the flashlight to let him see the digits.

I've been at this a couple of hours now. I was sure I'd find shelter before this.

He rested a bit more. *This porch is a shelter, isn't it? I'm not getting snowed on.*

A flake landed on his cheek to argue the point.

He sniffed. Then sighed. "Find shelter, then I can rest."

Staying Alive

Will walked out to the edge of the street and swept his flashlight beam in all directions. Other than noticing that the flashlight was fading rapidly, he did see another house, just the roof through the trees. He trudged on, the headache growing more noticeable with each step.

The flashlight showed little about the house, other than it was of a rustic wooden beam construction. He knocked and rattled the door, but it looked like he needed to go in through the window.

He unfastened a snowshoe and slammed the aluminum frame against the window. It just bounced off.

I didn't hit it hard enough.

He took off the other one and braced himself, swinging the pointy end against the glass. It cracked. Panting with exhaustion from the hard slog through deep snow, he hit the glass again until it broke.

Using the snowshoe, he knocked out the slivers of glass until there was an opening wide enough to crawl through.

...

Will lay panting, relishing the hard dry floor under him. He was tempted to take a little nap right where he lay. That is, until he felt the moisture on his arm.

The flashlight was nearly done for, but it showed the ripped sleeve of his snowmobile suit and the dark stain.

Oh, I cut myself. I'm in trouble now. These suits are expensive. Dad will make me pay for it.

But if he was bleeding, he needed to get that stopped.

He unzipped the front and slipped the top off his shoulder. He felt the sharp pain and the sticky mess the blood had made. Most of it was soaking into his long john tops.

When he tripped over the half-undone suit, he angrily kicked the rest of it off. It was cold in the dark place, but he had to be able to move around. He fished out his cell phone.

He'd never used it, but carried it along to take pictures. He powered it up and used the lit screen to let him see the room. He fumbled through some drawers in the kitchen until he found some towels.

With the cell phone propped up on the kitchen table, he was able to see the cut. He winced. It was a long and fairly deep cut, oozing blood. He took one of the smaller towels and tied it around his arm to put pressure on the wound.

That should stop the bleeding. I can do a better dressing when there's light.

But he was thirsty, very thirsty. He knew his water bottle was empty. He'd filled it twice during the course of the day, stashing it in an inside pocket to keep the water from freezing.

He pulled the crumpled bottle from his suit and checked the refrigerator. He'd seen several houses where the powerless refrigerator had insulated the food inside well enough that it hadn't frozen. Unfortunately, he didn't see anything drinkable in this one.

Sighing, he went over to the front door and unfastened the locks. Stepping out into the snow in just his jeans, he filled his bottle with fresh powder and came back inside. His teeth were chattering.

Hurriedly checking the closets, he found a couple of blankets and bundled himself and the bottle of snow, stretched out on the couch.

I hope I don't bleed on their couch. This all will be a mess to clean up tomorrow.

The water bottle stung his skin as he warmed it up with his body, but he needed to drink.

. . .

He woke in the dark, realized his water bottle now held water and he drank it down hurriedly. The headache was bad.

He also needed to pee. He fumbled for his cell phone, but he'd neglected to power it down. It was now dead—useless as a flashlight.

The room felt like ice, but there was just a faint glow through the windows, it was enough to fumble his way around the room, feeling the walls and finally locating the bathroom by touch. The toilet tank was empty, a reasonable precaution if you were going to leave a house empty in the winter. But he sat and emptied himself anyway. *Tomorrow, I'll take care of this.*

He closed the door and stumbled back to the couch and bundled himself up again.

...

The daylight stirred Will out of dream. Seeing the light banished the dream into oblivion. *Morning.* He adjusted the blanket to cover his nose. *Too tired. I'll sleep in.* It wasn't as if he could do much of anything yet.

The sneezing fit and the fierce headache told him he had a cold. *I just need to rest some more. Surely Mom would say that.*

A few hours later, he forced himself out to scrape up more clean snow to melt for water. The snowfall during the night had obscured his tracks. If anyone was looking for him, that might be a problem, but he couldn't deal with it. Getting water to drink and crawling back under the covers was his priority.

...

He huddled under the blanket, shivering. No amount of tucking or wrapping would make it comfortable.

I can't wait forever. I need to find a way to get warm.

Will looked around from his place on the couch. The fireplace had been swept clean of the ashes. He didn't see any wood. If there was some, then he'd have to bundle up and go outside to find it.

His bloody and torn snowmobile suit was crumped on the floor. He didn't even have a coat—just jeans and a long-sleeved shirt over his long underwear. He winced at his arm. Maybe he should just put his bloody underwear and shirt back on.

He frowned at the towel wrapped around his upper arm, stained dark red. No, he couldn't put his shirt over that, and he didn't dare risk losing more blood.

But I'll freeze without a fire, or without food to keep burning calories.

Weak, he stumbled over to the kitchen and rummaged through the pantry. He grabbed a box of Cheerios and brought it back to the couch. He munched the crunchy breakfast cereal, wishing for the sugar-coated versions just for the calories.

A bit later, he found a bag of charcoal briquettes in the pantry, along with a can of lighter fluid. It was obviously just for a BBQ grill probably hidden somewhere on the property, but it ought to burn anywhere. He dumped the whole bag, paper and all in the fireplace and soaked it with the fluid. One match started it going. He filled a couple of large cooking bowls with clean snow and let it melt on the hearth.

He wrapped himself in the blankets, huddled on the floor as close to the coals as he could safely manage. For a little while, he was warm.

...

What have I got? A cold, the flu, or something worse. Lily had pneumonia and coughed on me. Is that what I'm coming down with? Mom always had a name for my symptoms. I could never be bothered to learn the difference.

It would be pretty bad, stranded by himself in a house he couldn't keep warm. He'd been overdue for a day now. Maybe his parents wanted to find him, but he'd taken the snowmobile. Kelly was still at the hospital and needed to stay with her father. She probably thought he was still puttering around, doing his job.

No one knew where he was, and with the new avalanche somewhere south of town cutting off Hoosier Pass, finding one guy was hardly a high priority.

I told my parents I'd be okay. Even if I was stranded, I said I'd find shelter easy enough. I just didn't count on getting sick and injured.

He dipped a cup into the melted water and sipped. The charcoal was glowing red and made the water warm. It wasn't as tasty as cold water, but it warmed him up inside.

How long will this last? All the furniture is wooden. Should I break a chair and toss it into the fire?

The idea was distasteful. He was an uninvited guest in this house. It was bad enough he'd broken the window and smeared blood on the floor. It went against the grain to start smashing up the furnishings.

His arm ached and he shifted position a little. It seemed like it was getting a little colder. The daylight was gone and the center of his world seemed to be the red glow of the charcoal.

Maybe I should have made a smaller fire and held some of the charcoal back to keep it going longer. Too late now.

He closed his eyes and pulled the blankets around him even tighter. Gradually, the charcoal turned to ash. The red glow dimmed. Will slept fitfully in a house returning to the frozen temperature it had been before he disturbed it.

Nurse Kelly

Will had a strange dream about being pulled into a frozen pond by a giant beaver. He swatted it.

"Will! You're awake! Help me. You're too heavy to lift."

"Kelly?"

"Yes! Now put your arm here and help me lift you up onto the mattress."

Will was confused, but did as he was told. "Am I ... hospital?"

"No. Now lift this leg." With help, he rolled onto the bed.

He blinked away the blurriness in his eyes. "How did you get a bed in here?" He was still in the cabin, he could see that the fire he'd started had died, leaving just a pile of ash.

That's what his mouth felt like. "Water?" The bowls he'd left to warm by the fire were covered in ice.

"Here." Kelly held his head and helped him drink from a plastic water bottle. She said, "I just unfolded the couch. It's a sofa-sleeper."

The thought penetrated. *Stupid again. I should have known.* Probably most of the couches in these houses were fold-out beds.

He wanted to ask her more, but just as soon as he finished drinking, she was gone. It was daylight. When did she appear? Was she alone?

He tugged at the blankets. Nothing was warm—not the blankets and certainly not the mattress under him. But all he could do was curl up and try to shiver.

He must have dozed off again, because he woke to flickering orange flames. There was a roaring fire in the fireplace. Kelly was sitting on the mattress beside him, tugging at the towel knotted around his arm.

"A cut."

She frowned at him. "I can tell. There's blood all over the place. I need to look at it. Now don't fight me. Relax your arm."

He closed his eyes. It felt like his head was wrapped up in a blanket with some gnome pounding on it. Only when she pulled the towel free did the pain from the cut override the headache.

He grunted.

"Don't move your arm. I need to clean it good."

"The water is frozen."

"Not anymore. Just stay still."

She was right, because she was washing out the wound with warm water. How long had she been there?

He looked at her working, a frown on her face.

"Why are you here?"

She kept her eyes on her work. "Somebody had to hunt you down. Your parents were worried. They contacted the police and the police tracked me down, since they knew you brought me to the hospital."

She clenched her teeth as she hurriedly dabbed an ointment and wrapped gauze to hold the cut together.

"How did you find me?"

She shrugged. "It wasn't hard. I skied the road and found your snow-mobile. This was only the fourth house I checked. The broken window and the snowshoes on the porch gave it away."

"You skied here?"

"It's what I do. I told the police—but not your parents—that I had an idea where you might have sought shelter. They've got a big push going to clear the new avalanche and all their efforts are focused on that. It's a smaller avalanche on the other side of the town of Blue River."

Will nodded. "Gotta clear that."

"Supposedly, I was just going to ski the road, find you and let people know where you were."

He coughed. "How's your father?"

She sighed. "Better, but he's got complications. And now, I've got you to worry about as well."

She reached for her coat and pulled out her little blue radio. She pushed the buttons.

"Kelly? Is that you?"

"Yes, Dad. I'm fine. But can you call Nurse Lucy again?"

"Okay." There was a click.

Kelly said, "I've already sent word that I'd found you and word will get back to your parents."

"Hello, Kelly Winslow?"

"Yes, Lucy. I need more advice." She stood up. "The cut is deeper than I'm used to and it shows signs of infection."

Will couldn't quite hear the nurse's reply as Kelly walked over to the door and vanished into other parts of the house.

"I think I can find that. I saw ... Yes. Here it is."

Will listened but all he could hear was Kelly saying, "Yes. Okay. I think so."

He couldn't do anything but wait. *I'm useless again. I've really messed up. Now even Kelly has to take care of me.*

She showed up with a saucepan and put it on the fireplace to heat up.

"Between you and my father, I'm learning a lot more health care than I ever expected I'd need."

"Planning to become a nurse?" He tried to joke, punctuating it with a coughing fit.

"Oh, I hope not! If the snowmobile was running, I'd load you up and get you to the hospital. I'm not looking forward to this next part. What happened anyway?"

Will shook his head. "Stupidity. Either I ran out of gas or I added some really bad, old gas and it clogged the fuel line. I don't know exactly."

She looked over at the saucepan. "What would it take to get it running?"

He shrugged. "We could find some gas. Either a can somewhere or siphon from a stranded car. If the snowmobile starts up with new gas, then great. Otherwise we'd have to replace the fuel filter and that takes more tools and parts than we have here."

Kelly nodded thoughtfully. "And I'd have to be doing the work. You're sick, and I'm not letting you out of this place until you get a lot better. I can siphon gas, but anything with tools is probably beyond me."

Will nodded. "Me, too. I'd hate to take the snowmobile apart in the middle of a snowdrift wearing gloves."

She sighed. "The water is boiling. The next step is going to be tough."

"Oh?"

She nodded. "I've got to stitch up your cut." She gave him a sick grin. "Looking forward to having me stick a needle into you over and over again?"

"Ugh."

"That's my opinion." She picked up the saucepan and brought it close to the bed and set it on the side table. She had boiled the needle and thread. "Can you take it, or should I get a bungee cord to tie down your wrist?"

He realized she was serious. "Let's see if I can tough it out." This wasn't like a hospital where they could deaden the nerves before sticking him.

She went to the sink and with a pan of water she scrubbed her hands. Will watched with growing dread.

I can't blow this. I can't be a bad patient in addition to all my other failures.

He tried breathing slowly, as well as he could with his cough.

When she removed the gauze and cleaned the wound again, he tried to relax and close his eyes. But it was as if he could see everything anyway. The needle punched in and he gasped. She made the first stitch.

He nodded. "Go on."

Concentrating on other things, like his headache, or the feel of her hand holding his arm in place, he made it through with only a few outright cries of pain.

"It's done." She said, and he realized she had sweat on her forehead. It had been hard on her.

But then she had to fix the dressing again.

...

He woke when she was whispering into the radio again. She had an earphone plugged in.

"It's okay, Daddy. He's as weak as a kitten and I have to stay here to take care of him. I don't know if it's pneumonia or just a bad cold, but I can't risk letting him out in the weather just yet."

She nodded at his reply. "That's what I think, too. Besides, there's food here and enough firewood to keep us warm, maybe a couple of cords. It's more comfortable here than in your hospital room."

"But now, call the nurse, would you?"

He must have drifted off again, because Kelly woke him as she pulled his blanket off and laid down beside him.

"This is nice," he muttered.

"Don't get the wrong idea." She laid her head against his bare chest. "I don't have a stethoscope. Cough for me."

It wasn't hard. He coughed several times.

She sighed. "I'm listening for fluid in your lungs. I *think* you're okay. I'm supposed to be listening for crackles, at least that's what I've been told." She shook her head. "Maybe you've dodged pneumonia, if you behave yourself."

When she didn't move her head, he put his good arm on her shoulder and held her gently.

She didn't stir.

"Will, there's something I need to tell you."

House Rules

Other than being sick and injured, and feeling horrible about all the mistakes he'd made, Will was at peace, holding Kelly next to him.

"Go ahead. What do you have to say?"

She shifted her head slightly, whether to listen to his breathing or heart or just for comfort, he didn't know.

"Will, you know what I said about Beth?"

He tried to remember. "Um. She was looking for a boyfriend?"

"More than that. Beth *needs* to have a guy. It's so much a part of who she is that she'll easily risk going out with a bad guy rather than have no one at all.

"Well, I recognized that part of her very quickly when she came to room with me. It was very familiar, because it's just like my mother."

"Hmm." It was all he could say.

"I don't talk about my mother to other people. It's not something I want to talk about. But I need you to understand."

"Okay." He didn't know where she was going with this, but as long as he could hold her to his chest like this, he was content.

"I don't know how many guys my mother went with before she met Dad, but maybe because I showed up so quickly, she stayed longer than normal. She was my mother up until I was seven, but even then, she had an eye for other guys.

"I don't know why Dad put up with her, but they never really had an angry break up. She just left, and it was up to Dad to explain what a divorce was.

"Oh, they're still friends. She's Daddy's sponsor. He couldn't have competed in the Olympics without her money. She's the one who paid for our stay at the lodge this year. I think it's family money or something. I've never been led to expect that I'd ever inherit any of it, and I don't really want it.

"I want to be my own person. I don't want to be Mom, second edition. A long time ago, I decided I'd never chase after boys the way she did."

Kelly lifted her head and stared into his eyes by the flickering light of the fireplace. "Will, I have a rule. That story about Dad forbidding me to date ski bums was only partly true. My rule is that I'll never get serious—get really close to any guy I haven't known for a year."

He still had his arm around her, there alone together with her in a warm bed.

He sighed. "Well, like you told your dad. I'm weak as a kitten right now."

She giggled. "And I'm very glad of that. Otherwise I'd have to keep my distance."

He took a deep breath. "Um, refresh my memory. Did we meet one or two days before the solar flare? I'll need to put it on my calendar."

"So, you're okay with this?"

"I'll need more details. What does 'getting serious' and 'getting really close' actually mean? But yeah. You need to be who you want to be. I'd really love the chance to spend a year getting to know you better."

She laid her head back onto his chest. "We'll work it out. Before you, I sort of had a three-foot rule, but I've re-thought that one."

He stroked her hair. "Enjoy this while you can. I *am* a guy."

She nodded and slowly climbed out of bed. "But for now, I'm going to heat up some water for your bath. You need it. But you don't get personalized service."

He nodded. "I have sort of noticed the smell myself."

. . .

Will made do with a few inches of water in the tub and scooped about half of the rinse water into the toilet tank for a good flush.

From the results of Kelly's scavenging, he estimated that the owner of the house had to be over three hundred pounds. The jeans he borrowed needed his own belt to cinch up the excess. The borrowed shirt was saggy as well.

Kelly was soaking his blood-stained clothes in a soapy basin, stirring it with a ladle.

"I can do that."

She nodded and handed him the ladle. "Don't use your bad arm. Take it easy."

Hardly had he sat down beside the basin when she went to the pantry to find something to eat. "Mac and cheese?"

"Sounds wonderful."

He checked his watch by the light of the fire. "Is this Tuesday?"

"No, Wednesday."

He sighed. "I lost track."

She stirred the pot on the other side of the hearth. "In that logbook, do you have an idea where I can find some gasoline?"

"Oh, are you going to try to get the snowmobile running?"

"If I can. You need antibiotics, both for your cold and for your cut. I'd rather drive to the hospital than ski both ways. And if I can, I'd like to go by the lodge and ask your parents for a coat for you. I'm afraid your snowmobile suit is in pretty sad shape. I don't think I can sew it back up."

He tugged at the loose sleeve on the shirt he wore. "Mr. McGregor didn't leave a coat?"

"Nothing really heavy. Is that his name?"

"I was just guessing. I haven't felt like looking for records."

She tapped the spoon on the edge of her pot. "Let's get some food into you."

...

A little while later, she pulled out a foldable wooden drying rack and draped his washed clothes over it. His watch said nine in the evening when Kelly appeared in a large fluffy white nightgown, carrying a kerosene lantern.

"Mrs. McGregor left some things in the closet as well, but I keep tripping over this one."

Will chuckled. "It looks like it's ten layers thick."

"Almost. But that's perfect for this weather."

He watched as she scrubbed her clothes and wrung them out.

"I hope everything is dry by morning."

Will hoped so too. Nothing would be worse than damp clothes in freezing weather.

"I've been thinking," he said. "Mr. Severs, Lily's father, left the keys for their car at the house where they stayed. I'm pretty sure the car is in the attached garage. If you had a siphon hose and a gas can, that might be your best bet to get some gasoline for the snowmobile."

"The McGregors have a can, and I think I saw a garden hose curled up in their store room. I could cut it down."

"Have you ever siphoned gas before?"

"Not personally, but I've seen it done."

"The trick is avoiding swallowing any of it. You've gotta crimp the hose right after you suck and before it gets to your mouth."

By the light of the lantern, they reviewed his logbook and located the Severs house on the map.

She nodded, and then shook out her clothes and added them to the drying rack. Soon enough they were baking in the heat of the fireplace. She turned off the lantern.

Kelly dried her hands and then climbed into bed next to him. "I'll add wood to the fire and turn the rack in a little bit."

He put his arm around her as they waited under the blankets. "Just to keep our story straight—I slept in the bed and you slept on the couch?"

She chuckled. "Yes. And we were both fully clothed."

He winced in the darkness. "At least that part is true."

Her cold toes poked his warm feet. "In spite of the … circumstances, we're not really doing anything."

He sighed. "I know. This is nothing more than sitting together in a movie theater." He gave her a little squeeze.

She spoke quietly, "If everything goes perfectly—if I get the snowmobile started and return with warm clothes and antibiotics for you, then tomorrow night we'll be back at the lodge and back to keeping at arm's length. But I would like, someday, to go on a real movie date with you. Popcorn and all."

"Ahhh! Popcorn."

She laughed.

...

When Kelly shook him awake, he wasn't sure what he'd been dreaming about, but he felt like she'd been in them.

She was already dressed in her snow gear.

"I'm about ready to walk out the door, but I wanted to show you a couple of things."

He nodded and stepped barefooted on the cold wooden floor. *I need slippers.*

She led him to the back door out the side of the kitchen and pointed out where the firewood was stacked. "Don't stay out longer than a minute at a time. You can't risk getting chilled."

"Right. Do you have the map?"

She shook her head. "I'm sure where I'm going. I reviewed it already." She waved her cut-down garden hose. "I'm all set."

He sighed. "Be careful."

She smiled. "Out on skis in the snow is home territory for me. I'll be fine."

She went out the door, and he watched through the glass as she fixed her skis and scooted down, out of sight.

Exploring the House

Will watched out the front window for thirty minutes, worrying about her before he rummaged through the pantry for more breakfast cereal. He munched on the shredded wheat dry, not really anxious to heat up water to soak it in.

I can't just twiddle my thumbs here all day.

He checked his dried clothes. Both his long underwear tops and his shirt were torn and stained, in spite of being washed. But they were relatively clean and certainly dry. He changed out of the borrowed clothes and felt a little bit more like himself again. He added the oversized shirt as a light jacket and made a dash to collect more firewood. *I'm tired of being cold.*

After he built up the fire, he picked up his logbook and started touring the place, noting down resources, like he was supposed to.

I'll never keep track of all the things we've been using. But I need to do what I can.

Sadly, he was clearly underpowered. Before, he could have inventoried three or four houses like this before taking a break. Now, he had to go sit by the fire every fifteen or twenty minutes. The cough was annoying, too. But if Kelly was confident he wasn't coming down with pneumonia, that was a blessing.

He found the storeroom where there was a mangled garden hose and a pair of garden shears still out on the floor. He cleaned up the mess and noted down on his logbook the use of the hose.

The next room was dark, with no windows. He went back and lit the kerosene lantern and investigated.

He had to stare at the equipment for a bit before he puzzled out what it was.

There was a ragged logbook. He sat down at the table and by the light of the lantern thumbed through the pages.

Gene Barton (not named McGregor) was an amateur radio operator, and this was his equipment. At a glance, half of it was commercial and half looked like he'd built it himself.

His logbook showed that over the years, Gene had communicated with people from all over the world. *Like a big chat room, only you have to make your own equipment? Before the internet, it seems.*

He turned the page and there was a wiring diagram for the power system. "Off-Grid Power," it said.

Will's heartbeat picked up. Off-grid was exactly where he was. Could he make the radio work?

He moved the lantern a little closer and traced the lines with his finger. *Solar power? Generator A? Generator B? Gene thought big.* But was this a plan, or did he actually build it?

Start with the battery. He got the basic idea. Everything ran off the battery, and the various power sources charged the battery.

He carried the lantern slowly around the room. And there it was, or rather there they were. There were two large batteries, gathering dust, but obviously wired up to something. He found a rag and brushed the dust free.

"Two six-volt deep-discharge batteries. Are they charged?"

He looked around for something to test it with, but didn't see anything easy to use. Surely a guy like this had a voltmeter or something, but he'd have to find it.

"Where do the wires go?" On the chart, the wires on the output side went to an inverter to make house current. He quickly found the box, but clicking its power switch did nothing. "So, the batteries are dead."

He followed the other wires. He had to keep the rag handy. This off-grid power system hadn't been used in some time. This house, like all the others in this area was connected to Breckenridge's power. He'd been ducking under those power lines for days now.

Why did he need an off-grid system?

He turned some pages and found out why.

This sudden five-foot snow and being trapped here with no power for a week is the pits. I'm going to make me an alternate power system. At least one good enough to run my radios, some lights, and just maybe the microwave. I'll have to see how expensive it is.

I know Fred's RV has a power system he can use without having to run his generator. I'll need to talk to him, once the county gets their snowplows out to clean things up!

Will nodded. Now he just had to find out how to make it work.

But with that in mind, he kept tracing the wires. Soon he found a switch that connected the radio gear either to a plug on the wall, or the output of the inverter.

Oops. Were the radios fried when the solar flare happened? If so, this is all useless.

He flipped the power to the inverter side. Not that it made any difference. There wasn't any power on either systems.

"Let's track those generators."

. . .

Will raced to the front porch when he heard the snowmobile. It was already near sundown and he had been checking for her arrival every few minutes since noon. He'd been through every worst-case he could think of, including getting shot by that guy with the gun.

His heart was racing as the snowmobile pulled up to the porch.

"Did you miss me?" She beamed at him.

He smiled at the skis she always had with her. He was glad of that. Better skis than those snowshoes he'd relied on.

"I was worried. I even worked up a timeline and made guesses as to how long each leg would take."

She dug out two bags strapped to the snowmobile. "Go back inside. I don't want you to get chilled."

He took the bags and made her sit down in front of the fire. "Tell me all about it."

She peeled off her gloves and cap and rubbed her hands in front of the fire.

"I found the Severs' place okay, but siphoning the gas was a lot harder than it looked. I even got a mouthful of gasoline I spit right out. Yuck! I found some powdered tea I mixed up to get rid of the taste. I hope it doesn't kill me in a few years."

He laughed. "It hasn't killed me yet. But after the first time I made that mistake, I stuck to using special siphon hoses with a hand pump."

"I want one of those, just to keep handy."

She went to the pantry. "I knew there was this hot chocolate mix, and I promised myself I'd treat myself when I made it here."

"I'll mix it for you. Stay by the fire."

She hesitated, then turned the box over to him. He scooped up some fresh show to melt and listened to her story as the pot heated on the hearth.

Kelly unzipped her jacket as she warmed up. "Skiing while carrying a can of gasoline is no fun, I tell you. But, I found the snowmobile and brushed off all the new snow. I added the gas, and then tried to get it to start."

"Tried? There was a problem."

She nodded. "You said there might have been some bad gas, and I think you're right. It started rough, and then died. I went through that four or five times before it ran smoothly, and even then, when I tried to drive off, it only ran at slow speed for a bit, and then suddenly, Boom! It popped smoke out the tailpipe. But after that, it ran fine."

She gestured as she talked, and he grinned, keeping an eye on the pot of water.

"So, back to the Severs' place to get more gas. I wasn't about to run out on the way down the hill."

"How much gas did you carry the first time?"

"Just a gallon. I figured more was a waste. Either the engine would run or it wouldn't.

"So, more siphoning, and I had gotten it down by then. I added five more gallons before heading off. I took the downtown route and stopped off at the sheriff's office to report in before they started worrying about us again. Then, off to the hospital.

"I checked in with Dad. He's about the same, but in no danger now. I talked to Nurse Lucy about your condition and she talked to the doctor. I've got some pills for you to take and an antibiotic ointment for your cut."

Will checked the water, but it wasn't warm enough yet. He nodded. "Go on."

She sighed. "Then I drove to the lodge and told them all about your cut and how you really needed a better coat before I tried to bring you back to town."

"And what did they say?"

She winced a little. "Well, there were a few probing questions, especially about us spending the night together. I gave them the official story, and left out all the seedy details. I mean it was plain that I liked you—I didn't even try to hide that—but I insisted we're just casual friends. Nothing physical at all."

"And did they buy it?"

"Hard to tell. But, your Mom was quick to put together a change of clothes for you and your best coat. I've got them in that bag. They didn't actually accuse us of anything, but I could sense some reservations."

She waved her hands. "And that's it. Your father insisted on topping the gas tank all the way up, and he *almost* insisted that he come rescue you instead of me. I stonewalled him. I knew where you were, but I couldn't point it out on a map."

"I'm surprised he let you win."

She nodded. "The thing is, there was some crisis at the lodge he had to deal with. Some kid went missing."

"Missing? Who?"

"Rick somebody. You know him. He had that hand-crank charger?"

Will frowned. She asked, "Do you know where he went?"

"I'm not sure." *Dare I betray his secret? I'm part of this. Or am I? He never knew I'd delivered his love letter. I never had the chance to tell him.*

Will nodded. "He was wanting to go back to the mobile home park to look for something. But his family knew that. That's my only guess. I wonder if he hitched a ride with someone. That's a long walk back to the avalanche. He was trying to get me to take him on the snowmobile."

Kelly nodded. "And someone would have seen him walking. But there's nothing we can do about it now."

She smiled, "So, after you take your medicine and I check your wound, are you ready to bundle up and go home? We'll arrive after dark, but I think we can handle it."

Will shook his head. "There's something I need to show you first."

Radios

Will held the kerosene lantern as they entered the dark room. He reached over and flipped a switch. LEDs lit up, doubling the light.

"What is this?" Kelly asked.

"Mr. McGregor's real name is Gene Barton, and he was an amateur radio operator. This is his radio gear."

"And he has electricity?"

"Sort of. I've been trying to get this stuff to work." He sat down on an stationary bike, a modified Schwinn exerciser and started pedaling. The LED lights brightened up somewhat.

Speaking louder over the noise of the bike, he continued, "He had regular power, but when a big snowstorm hit and isolated him without power for a week, he built an off-grid power system for his radio. I guess he never really needed it. So most of this, like this pedal-power generator, was just idle and covered with dust. I found connectors for a gasoline powered generator, but the generator itself is gone. And supposedly, there are solar panels on the roof, although I suspect they are buried under the snow."

He stopped pedaling and pointed to the LEDs. "The only thing running directly from the batteries are those lights. The radio gear runs off an inverter."

He flipped another switch, there was a buzz, and a big metal box the size of a microwave lit up. Will tuned a big knob and from the speaker a voice was reporting on a flooding rescue in Northern California. "Stay connected, stay informed, KOMO radio."

The lights flickered, the buzz died, and the radio went dark.

Will shrugged. "I haven't charged the batteries well enough to keep the radio running long."

She said, "But some parts of the country have power."

"Yeah. I think that's a Seattle station. I've just been tuning the dial randomly. We can get news. And that's valuable. But this other gadget here is a transmitter. If I could get it working, maybe we could call for help. Does anyone really know how bad off we are here in the mountains? How bad is it in other parts of Colorado?"

He looked at Kelly. "I think maybe I'd like to stay here a bit longer and see if it's just a pipe dream or if we could make contact with someone who could help."

Kelly nodded thoughtfully. "I understand, and I agree, but you've got to take your medicine and then we've got to use my *little* radio to let Dad and the folks down in the valley know that I won't be coming home again tonight." She gave him a grin. "I'm sure that'll go over well."

. . .

"Daddy, you really shouldn't get upset." She cradled her little blue gadget against her hear, talking softly. "Will and I have an understanding, and there's nothing going on like you're worried about. We just have to stay here longer because of this big radio Will has discovered. It's important."

She nodded. "Yes, I know, Dad. I love you, too. But, now, your job is to get the sheriff's office to call us back on your radio. There's some things we need to talk about with them. Can you do that for me?"

There were some more conversation that Will couldn't follow because she was talking too quietly. When he realized that it was family stuff, he didn't try to listen, turning his attention to the pantry. The canned food was a little old, but nothing he'd worry about.

When she ended the call, he held up a can of mushroom soup. "Any preferences for supper?"

"That sounds great. You start a pot with water added. I need to change. I'm sweating."

She took one of the bags and went into the bedroom. *It is pretty warm in here. I'm probably using up the firewood too fast.* It was just a welcome change of pace to wear just a shirt and jeans without layers of heavy underwear and a jacket all the time.

He heard her coming back as he stirred the pot. "You brought a change of clothes? Did you expect to stay the night?"

When he looked up, she was smiling, dressed in light blue exercise clothes.

"I just had a couple of minutes to grab something at my place, just in case. I knew I was running late and if your health had gotten worse, I wasn't about to pull you off the mountain in the dark."

He nodded. "Reasonable." It was nice to see her in girl curves, rather than in ski gear. She was covered up enough her father shouldn't have anything to gripe about.

She took over the stirring, and sipped the mix. "Get a couple of bowls and spoons."

They relaxed by the fire, appreciating the soup. Will appreciated the companionship. Every day with Kelly felt like a date, and he had so little experience at that.

She took the bowls to the sink and rinsed them. "Since I'm dressed for it, I figured I'd try out that exercise bike. Are there any special switches I need to know about?"

"I'll go with you."

They lit up the room and she hit the bike. "Are the LEDs wasting juice?" she asked.

"Just a trickle. Don't worry about that. The real power hogs are those radios. From what I can see, that transmitter has tubes instead of transistors. It's really old." He picked up the logbook and moved the chair where he could see her work when he looked up from the pages.

"What are you reading?"

"Gene Barton had a log book, more than one from what I see on the shelves. He wrote down things about his radio, like the power system. But he also wrote down every time he talked to someone over the radio. He listed the time and date, their call sign, and the frequency. Sometimes he noted down other settings as well."

"Call sign?"

"Yes. He was a licensed radio operator, so he had a call sign W5KZZ."

"Like a radio station."

"Right. He *was* a radio station. And the people he talked to had call signs as well. They even had special post cards."

He stood up and picked up a stack of cards on a small rack. He thumbed through them, post cards of all sizes and shapes. "This one is from Albania. This one is from Brazil. England, Canada, Japan." He chuckled as he puzzled out the hand-written notes. "They all look custom designed. Everybody made their own cards and exchanged them with people they met over the air."

He carefully stacked them back together and put them back where he found them.

She said, "Sort of like the internet."

"Yes, but without any help, no wi-fi to connect to, no jack to plug into. They built their own equipment and made their contacts. It's fascinating. Reaching out across the world and not knowing who you're going to contact, what country they're in, or even what language they speak. All you know is that they've got some kind of radio like you do. Before the internet, that must have been something."

She nodded as she pedaled. "And now, we don't have the internet either."

"Right. No internet, no telephones, not even any roads to travel either. Something like this radio right here might be the only way we can contact the outside world."

...

After reading for a while, Will said, "I'm going to test a few things, now that you've charged it up so much."

She sighed and let the generator come to a standstill. "I think I'm going to go fix some tea. You want some?"

"That would be great."

Will flipped the inverter on. The buzz was less noticeable this time. *Probably it buzzes when the battery power is low.*

The radio came back on and with just a slight tweak of the big knob, the news broadcast came back on. He listened with half his attention as he compared the obscure notes in the logbook with the physical knobs and buttons on the radio.

Some of the settings were obvious. One was the frequency. On the receiver, he could read the radio frequency on a digital readout and there was a band setting which clicked through five different frequency ranges. A little experimentation made him confident that he could find a given frequency.

However, he had no idea what CW meant, nor SSB, although there was an SSB switch on the radio.

One contact to someone in Denver had the notation; 40m, CW, 7.022. He suspected the 7.022 was the frequency, but what was 40m and the CW?

Kelly came back with the tea and handed him a mug. "I'm going to pedal for a little bit more, then I'm going to go to sleep. It's been a big day for me."

"I didn't mean for you to take on the hard part," he said. "I'll be pedaling more tomorrow."

He was about half through with the tea when there was a chime. Kelly pulled her feet off the pedals. "That's my radio. It's late for Dad to call."

She hurried to the other room and answered it. With a frown she handed it over to Will.

"Hello?" Will had to get used to the push-to-talk button. This wasn't a telephone where both of you could talk at the same time.

"Is this Will Parker?" It sounded like Thompson, but before Will could answer, Sam Winslow answered, sounding like he'd just woken up. "This is Sam. Who is this?"

Will quickly pressed the button. "I'm Will. There are three of us."

There was a little confusion, and then Sam said, "If you don't want me, I'm signing off."

Thompson said, "Good night Mr. Winslow. I didn't mean to bother you."

Will spoke. "You've got your own FRS radio, then."

Thompson came back. "Yes. We had one in the desk. When I got a radio call that you wanted to talk to me, I dug it out and found out what channel to use from the hospital. What did you want to contact me about?"

"A couple of things actually. First, the owner of the house where I'm staying has an amateur radio room, complete with a transmitter. Have you guys found a way to communicate outside of Summit County yet? Over."

Thompson sighed. "Not really. We can talk to other of our cars on the other side of the avalanche, but Frisco, Silverthorne, and Dillon are cut off, too.

"I've sent messages—letters—with the cars that went hunting for food and fuel, but Park County is nearly as isolated as we are.

"Are you saying you can communicate with that radio you found?"

"We can certainly listen. I've been following the news. Some parts of the country have power, but they keep referring to the 'dark zones'. I suppose that means places like us. Over."

"But you haven't tried to transmit yet?"

"Sir, I'm just going through the logbook of the man who owns the gear. I hope to figure it out. The other complication is that we're working off of a pedal-power generator. Everything runs off a big twelve-volt battery. Two sixes, actually. Kelly is getting her exercise. But, I hope to try it tomorrow. Over."

Thompson said, "That would be a big help, if we could contact the DHSEM. Um. Over."

"Who's that? Over."

"Department of Homeland Security and Emergency Management. State-level coordinators for disaster stuff. FEMA is the federal ones. So, yes, if you can find a way to call them, it would be a great help. Over."

"Okay, then that's what we'll try to do. I'll call you on this channel the instant we learn how. Over."

"Great. And what was the other thing you wanted to ask me?"

Pillow Talk

"Sir, did the lodge ask for your help trying to find Rick Torino? Over."

Thompson hesitated a few seconds before replying, "Yes. Unfortunately, we don't have the manpower to do much of a search and no one seems to know where he is. Over."

"I just wanted you to know that Rick was very concerned about getting back to the mobile home park, even after I explained that his home was buried with snow. He tried hard to convince me to take him there on my snowmobile. I turned him down, but I wonder if he hitched a ride with someone else.

"I've been thinking about it since I heard he was missing, and I thought, maybe he'd tagged along with the snow clearance team—he'd get to the Swan Mountain avalanche and walk the rest of the way. What do you think? Over."

Kelly was listening carefully to the conversation and seemed to be puzzled.

Thompson replied, "Well, if he tried that, then that's a problem. The snow clearance team was sent to work on the southern avalanche and they're staying in houses in the town of Blue River. If he got caught up in that team, he might be tied up for days. But I suppose it wouldn't hurt to check with the mobile home park. Over."

"Then check with the Pattersons. I visited there recently and they seem to know who is who there at the park. Over."

"Patterson? Isn't there a guy your age named Patterson? Over."

"Yeah. Doug Patterson, and he has a sister Mary that's a couple of years younger. Over."

"Hmm. One more task to look into. But keep working on that radio. If we could get some help from Denver, it would make all the difference in the world. Over and out."

"Will do."

As he handed back Kelly's radio, she asked, "Hmm. So you know something about Rick Torino?"

"Just a little."

"A little more than you told the sheriff, I bet."

"Nothing I can share."

She nodded. "So there is a secret. So that means a girl is involved. If I can sense that, then so can Thompson. Is it that Mary Patterson? And she's sixteen, like Rick. I'm getting a Romeo and Juliet vibe here."

Will shook his head. "I hope not. That one didn't end well."

. . .

Will put in thirty minutes on the bicycle just out of sense of duty, although Kelly griped about how he was supposed to be resting to recover from his injury. After that, they shut down the lights, stoked up the fire, and settled in for the night.

He admired her nightgown without saying anything. He wished he could afford to change into something soft and comfortable as well, but shirt and jeans were his uniform as long as he was sharing the bed with her.

Kelly turned her head. "Okay, spill. What's the story about Rick and Mary? I can't stop thinking about it."

"I ... shouldn't."

"Oh, posh! This is pillow talk. I'm not going to spill any secrets."

Will was conflicted, but this was Kelly whispering in his ear. He sighed.

"Rick and Mary lived in the same mobile home park and they had some kind of secret thing going. And it was secret—from everyone. Certainly from their families. I could tell Rick was on the edge after being away from her for a few days. I told him I couldn't take him there, but I'd pass a message. He seemed content with that.

"So right after I dropped you off at the hospital when your Dad was doing poorly, I stopped at the mobile home park and made up a story about the Torinos and the other families that had been relocated to the lodge were

194

concerned with those that remained and Doug made me a list of who was left and how they were doing.

"You should have seen Mary, when I passed her the letter. She didn't even blink. It was as if she'd been passing secret messages forever. Obviously it wasn't something Rick had made up in his head. She was definitely in on it as well.

"Of course, with the snowmobile troubles, I never got to deliver Doug's list. Rick never heard that I'd delivered his message to Mary. I worry that he got so desperate that he did something dangerous."

Kelly gave his hand a squeeze. "It's not your fault. I can sympathize, though. I don't know what I'd do if something separated me from someone I loved. It doesn't matter what age you are when you click with someone."

Will got the feeling she wasn't just talking about Rick and Mary. Kelly had been thrown into his life by this disaster, and they weren't even discussing what would happen if life went back to normal. Kelly and her father were only living at the lodge for the ski season.

Will worried. If he and the girl next to him couldn't progress beyond being really good friends until a year had passed, where did that leave them when it came time for the Winslow family to move on?

He returned her squeeze of the hand, resisting the urge to pull her close. *Rick, I'm jealous. No matter how it plays out, you took your chance and acted on it. I'm a dummy, sleeping next to a beautiful girl who decided to trust me, and I can't do anything more than hold her hand.*

It was a long time getting to sleep. Beside him, Kelly stirred as well, whether from dreams or thoughts of her own, he couldn't tell.

...

In the middle of the night, Will woke, a little disoriented at having Kelly beside him. He stared at her face, illuminated by the glowing coals, her cheek half hidden by her hair. Then he eased out of bed.

With a little leftover tea, he crept into the radio room. His headache spiked when he turned on the LEDs, but he had a lot of reading to do.

His hunch turned out correct. There were other books hidden on the shelves, in among the logbooks. The ARRL Handbook was a godsend.

So much for CW. Even with the code chart in front of me, I'd never be able to send code at a usable speed, and listening to it is out of the question.

He found the key to some of the puzzles. "40m" was forty meters, an alternate way to talk about the frequencies. It was the wavelength of radio waves in the 7 megahertz range. The radio operators, Hams they called themselves, had various bands, all referenced by their wavelength. Each section of the band was reserved for different kinds of transmissions. CW, for "continuous wave", was for Morse code. "Phone" was what he was expecting, where you talk into a microphone. There was also "packet radio" which could actually handle internet communications.

SSB meant "single-sideband", which he didn't understand, but it was a thing. Both sides had to use it or not.

He looked over the radios again, with the handbook in hand, getting clear in his mind what was what.

"What are you doing?" Kelly, looking a bit bedraggled, was in the door.

"I couldn't sleep." He smiled. "I'm doing more research. It's the only useful thing I can do."

She leaned against the door sill, a distraction wiping all the technical info right out of his mind. "It's not dawn yet. You need your sleep."

"You go back to sleep. I'll nap later. I think I'm on to something here."

She nodded, holding herself steady, she looked sad. "Could … could I get a hug? I've had a bad dream."

He set down the book and walked over, putting his arm around her and holding her gently. "I'm sorry."

She shook her head. "It's not your fault. Just a lot happening lately."

He helped her back to the bed and tucked her in. He added a couple of logs to the fire and then went back to the radio room, careful to close the door so the light of the LEDs wouldn't disturb her sleep.

A lot happening. Yes, especially true for her. With a missing mother and a father in the hospital, she's on her own.

It made a little more sense now. It wasn't reasonable for a girl to trust a guy she'd just met as much as Kelly seemed to trust him. Spending the night alone with him—even sharing a bed. It was just that she needed *someone* to be close to.

And it made it all the more important that he stick to the straight and narrow. *What a ridiculous situation to be caught up in! If I saw it on TV or in a movie, I'd never believe two teens caught up in this dilemma could make it through the night without even a kiss.*

Just his luck.

He opened the book and forced his mind back on things technical. Amateur radio was supposed to be for people who had studied and passed a test proving they were competent in this. He'd never get the radio to work if he didn't understand it more.

This is hardly a consumer electronics gadget like a cell phone, where all the guts of the radio are hidden behind colorful buttons.

He chuckled. There was a chart of Q-codes Gene had printed off of Wikipedia. Shortcut codes to simplify communications. Some made sense. Some were too technical for him, and some were just funny.

QNB — "How many buttons on your radio?" "QNB 100/5" means that there are 100 buttons and I know what 5 of them do.

I guess some of the Ham radio guys had to start out ignorant too.

Calling Anyone

"Will, can you turn on that news station? I'm not a big news nerd, but it would be nice to hear something about the outside world."

He looked at the beads of sweat on her forehead. She'd tackled another round on the exercise bicycle and she certainly deserved to enjoy the fruits of her labor. He started the inverter and switched on the receiver. A little tuning found a morning news broadcast.

He flipped a different switch and the sound changed. "Gene put in house speakers so he could listen to the radio even out on the porch."

Will sighed. "If you don't mind, I'm going to take a little nap before I try to transmit, but I'd like to listen in as well. It's still a little early for transmitting and I'd hate to miss a contact because someone was still asleep or eating breakfast."

She nodded. "That's fine. When should I wake you?"

He shrugged. "I'll wake up. And this is not an expectation that you'll pedal the whole time. I'll do my part as well."

She sniffed. "I probably have stronger legs than you do."

He nodded. "You might at that." He had given her legs some examination when she wasn't watching. She was a skier. Of course his arms were probably stronger than hers, with all the snow shoveling he'd done.

After checking the fire and making sure there was fresh snow to melt for drinking and wash water, he stretched out on the bed and closed his eyes.

It's strange to think that the solar storm is old news in parts of the world.

Still from the various new stories, he could get a sense of where the dark zones, sometimes called dark territories, *weren't*. Hollywood was releasing new movies. There were scandals in Washington DC and New York City. When the world went dark, and there weren't enough replacement power transformers to go around, certain predictable places were first in line to get their power grids back up.

Then, there was a short feature mentioning the dark territories. They mentioned the transformer shortage, just like Lloyds had predicted. In the USA, the dark zones were mainly in the western states, where the population density was low. Cities got preference.

But some countries were entirely without power. The Lloyds prediction put a maximum two year expectation for power. Hearing the list of places still without a working power grid made him think they might have been optimistic.

There was a one-sentence comment about how the heavy snowfall in the Rocky Mountains was complicating recovery.

Will shook his head. "Tell me about it."

...

"Will," she shook his arm. "Wake up."

"What?" He frowned when he saw her dressed in her outdoor gear. He sat up.

"What's up?"

Her face was lined with worry. "My radio. Dad has had another relapse. I have to go back to the hospital."

Will pulled her close and gave her a deep hug. "I'll be fine. I completely understand that you need to be there. I'm sure your presence will help him pull out of it."

She nodded. "It's just so .... I'm worried."

"Then go. Hurry down. Only ...."

She pulled out the little blue gadget. "I know. You need the radio here. I won't need it."

He took it and set it aside to concentrate on her. "Did they give you any details?"

She shook her head. "Last time, they had to change medicines. I'm not a doctor. I have no idea."

He walked her out to the snowmobile and helped her brush off the fresh snow. He tapped the gas gauge, and it looked three-quarters full. "Don't take any risks. Don't jump any ravines."

She gave him a faint smile, then put on her goggles and started the engine. He watched as she drove off, then hurried inside.

...

Kelly had turned off the radio but left the inverter on. Will turned everything off and spent several long minutes pedaling to charge up the battery.

"I'm just wasting time." It was a complicated task. He was afraid of messing it up.

Noted in his own logbook were several contacts Gene had made to people in Denver. His best bet was to concentrate on those frequencies and settings and hope he made contact with one of them.

He powered everything back up and then sat down in the chair and centered the microphone in front of him. He tuned the receiver to the frequency from the notes and listened. He turned off the house speakers. That was just a waste of power.

There was a lot of static, and he could tell that there were people talking—lots of conversations overlapping each other. Some were distorted. He wondered. Just as an experiment, he flipped the SSB switch and tuned with a smaller knob. Indeed, some of those distorted conversations were now clearer.

He turned off the SSB and double-checked the original frequency. He set the transmitter to the same frequency and powered it up.

There was a big beige push-to-talk button on the microphone. He'd looked at the wires and it did something to switch between the receiver and the transmitter. It made sense you wouldn't want to be listening to a faint signal and suddenly transmit high power right on top of it.

He took a deep breath and pressed the button. Something in the transmitter hummed.

"Um. This is Breckenridge Colorado, trying to contact someone in Denver. Over."

He let up the switch and listened. There didn't appear to be any change. If anyone heard him, he was being ignored.

He pressed the button and repeated his call. No response.

I can't expect people to be on-call every minute of the day, waiting for a random person to call.

Will tried several more times before switching to a new frequency and trying again. There were definitely people out there, but nobody was paying him any attention.

Or I could be doing it wrong.

He worked it more than forty-five minutes before he heard the sound of the inverter buzz. He'd used up his battery.

He sighed, turned off the radios and inverter, and sat down to pedal more juice into the battery.

He'd only been at it a couple of minutes when there was a chime.

Kelly's radio!

He hurried into the other room and picked up the blue gadget from the bed.

"Hello, this is Will."

"Kelly here. I just wanted you to know that I'm at the hospital and that Dad is stable. Over."

"Good to hear. Any details from the doctors?"

"Not really. Last night he was struggling with his breathing, apparently and they have him on supplemental oxygen. The problem is that they have limited supplies. There's an electric thing that boosts the oxygen in the air, but...limited electricity."

He waited for her to say "over", but then he just talked anyway. "You hang in there."

"Yeah, I know. I just wish I could do *something*. Being helpless is killing me."

Will knew exactly how she felt.

"Will? How is the radio coming? Have you tried it yet? Over."

"Yes, I've been trying, but I haven't been able to make contact yet. Over."

He didn't want to mention that he'd burned through all the effort she'd put into charging the battery. That was not what she needed to hear right now.

"Oh." She sounded disappointed. "Well, keep at it. The doctors are worried about their dwindling medicine supplies. I know they want to try new medicines for Dad, but they are out. Over."

"I'll make it work, somehow. You just concentrate on being there to support your father. Hold his hand."

He wanted her to know, even thought he couldn't say it on the radio where Thompson and maybe other people could listen in, that he was there with her in spirit. Maybe they couldn't hold each other's hand right now, but he wanted her to know she wasn't alone."

"Okay, Will." He heard her sniff. She'd been crying. "I'll do my part. You do yours. Over."

"And I've got to get back to it. I'll talk to you soon. Over and out."

He clipped the radio to his belt. *Now how do I do my part? The radio isn't working.*

Checking the Connections

Will worked up a sweat, stripping off his shirt as he pedaled hard to get the battery charged. After an hour by his watch, he powered up the radio and tried again, repeating the frequencies he had culled from Gene Barton's logbook.

After several fruitless tries, he heard a repeating call as he tuned the receiver.

"CQ CQ CQ calling anyone in the Western US. CQ CQ CQ."

Hurriedly, Will tuned the transmitter to the same frequency and replied.

"This is Will Parker in Breckenridge Colorado! Can you hear me?"

He breathlessly listened, but the CQ caller hadn't heard him.

After his third attempt to make contact, the battery gave out again.

Will sagged over the microphone.

Why can't I make this work! It's impossible!

God! I can't fail at this. Not after Kelly....

He sat up and reached for the handbook again. *There has to be something I've missed.*

The blue radio on his belt chimed. He picked it up.

"Kelly?"

"No, this is Thompson. I was just checking in to see if you've managed to make any contact with that ham radio?"

Will sighed. He pressed the button. "No, sir, not yet. I've made several attempts, but I've currently run out of electricity again. I have to pedal on the bicycle generator for a while to get enough juice to power the radios. Over."

"Oh. Well, keep at it a little while longer. I've asked around to see if anyone has any experience with ham radio, but I haven't come up with anyone.

"And by the way, Rick Torino was in the snow clearance crew. Whether he meant to volunteer or not, he's now handling a show shovel full time. When I asked if there was some one who could keep an eye out for him, Nick Patterson agreed, since he knew the Torino family. I've notified Rick's family at the lodge. Over."

"Thanks. Good to know. And I'm not done trying to make this radio work. Too much depends on it. Over."

"I'm glad to hear it. Your folks are worried about you and if you can't get it to work, then we need to see about getting you back home. Over."

"Give me a little more time. It'll be worth it if I can crack this puzzle. Over."

"Okay then. Well, I've got other people waving at me. I'll check back later. Then. Out."

Will held the handset and was about to put it away when he noticed a flicker on the little screen.

He pressed the button. "Kelly? Did you catch that last conversation?"

"Yes. Sorry to eavesdrop, but it was interesting. Especially the news about Rick. Over."

"Yes. Interesting news about Rick and Nick Patterson. I'm sure Rick's folks were glad to hear the news. Over."

"Yes. Good news. And Dad was glad to have me here. I've got some things to do. Over."

"Me, too. And a lot of pedaling. Out."

Very interesting news about Rick. I wonder what he thinks about it, working side by side with Mary's father. I guess that depends on how much Nick Patterson knows or suspects about his daughter's romance. Interesting times for Rick.

Will stared at the little handset in his hand. How nice it would be if the ham radio was as simple to operate as this one. *QNB 5/5* Of course there were menu items controlled by those buttons that he hadn't explored. But it was simple enough to hand to a child for a day's play out on the slopes.

Just a simple slab of plastic with a stub of an antenna and a push-to-talk button.

He stared at it more intently, then picked up the ARRL Handbook. The logo of the Amateur Radio Relay League was right there on the cover,

206

a lozenge shape with the A at the top, Rs on each side, and the L at the bottom. In the middle was a simplified radio—an antenna at the top, a coil in the middle, and a ground at the bottom. He'd recognized the symbols from some of the pages he'd read in the handbook.

Looking over at Gene Barton's radio gear, he considered how complicated it looked, but the basics were all the same, whether ham radio, a FRS handset, or a cell phone.

The consumer electronics industry had made great technical advances, but it was invented in private radio rooms like this one. Hidden beneath the plastic, there were undoubtedly more sophisticated circuits like computers to make it user friendly, but the radio was the core.

He got off the exercise bicycle and carefully moved the receiver to where he could look at the connectors at the back.

Power cord. That's the speaker connection. And that's the antenna terminals.

He hadn't consider the antenna before. Cell phones had antennas so small they were hidden inside the case. Kelly's radio had just a simple innocuous stub. But the ham radio needed more, right? He traced the coax cable over to where it joined the transmitter. There was a switch box that was supposed to connect both the transmitter and receiver to the same antenna feed.

But right there, Gene had left things disconnected. The receiver was connected via a simple alligator clip to a string of wire that ran long two sides of the room along the ceiling join. The transmitter wasn't connected to anything. The cable to an outside antenna was clipped to the metal frame. *Why? Lightning protection maybe?*

But if he was interpreting things correctly, the transmitter couldn't transmit because it didn't have an antenna, and that handbook and made a big deal about how to make antennas. They had to be the right length for the bandwidth, and there were passive reflectors to help aim the signal and plenty of stuff he'd have to study awhile before he understood the math of it.

But surely Gene had the right kind of antenna, somewhere outside.

Carefully, he unclipped what he assumed was the outside antenna feed and connected it to the switch box. He screwed the receiver coax into its port.

Everything looked okay.

Will this do it?

He flipped the inverter on. He didn't have much battery life yet, but this should tell him if he was on the right track.

He turned on the receiver and adjusted the tuning knob.

There was nothing. No voices. Not even much static.

He flipped off the inverter.

Okay, I changed the antenna, but the outside one is worse than this little bit of wire.

Still that was *obviously* the outside antenna feed.

"I'll need to go outside and look at it."

Through the front window he could see a few flakes in the sky. It was still cold, still freezing outside. *And I might just have to climb up on the roof.*

"I'd better button up."

He looked longingly at the fireplace that had kept him warm and toasty for a long while now.

His coat and clothes were scattered about. *Long underwear, too.*

There was the bag Kelly had brought from the lodge. Stuff his mother had packed for him. Had she packed him extra underwear?

He dumped it all out on the bed.

A small box rolled out with the clothes. He picked it up and read the label. "Mom!"

It was a package of condoms.

He sat down on the bed and stated at it in his hand.

"What were you thinking?"

Thoughts churned in his head.

They thought Kelly and I were having sex, and this was just protection to keep her from getting pregnant. They never trusted me to keep my hands to myself in spite of what I said.

Or maybe, they liked Kelly and how she was taking care of me. Is this a subtile hint that maybe they wouldn't mind having her as a daughter-in-law? Maybe just Mom. She packed the bag. Maybe Dad wasn't even aware.

He tossed the box back onto the bed and stretched out, staring at the wood-beam ceiling. "This doesn't change anything."

He still needed to make the radio work and get help for Breckenridge and Kelly's father. He still was just a high school student that just might not graduate because of this stupid blackout. Kelly was still likely to move back to wherever she called home once the roads were cleared and the gas stations could pump gas.

And he couldn't push Kelly to change her one-year time limit. He didn't even want to change how she thought about herself. And when she did leave, he wanted her to think of him as the only guy in the world she could trust. She might even come back. Breckenridge was a great ski place.

"So why am I staring at the ceiling? I need to get to work."

He picked up the box of condoms.

I'm not telling anyone about this. I won't tell Kelly. I won't mention this to my parents. I'll just stuff it away for some day in the future.

All this really said was that his parents recognized that he wasn't a little kid anymore. It was up to him to prove that he was competent and responsible.

He stuffed it back in the bag and started laying on as many warm clothes as he could manage.

Eve

Staring at the roof from a dozen yards away, he could barely see the antenna. But since he knew what it was supposed to look like from the pictures in the handbook, he could see a couple of aluminum stubs sticking out of the snow.

Was it not working because it was buried in the snow? It was possible. Maybe there was enough melt in the snow from the warm roof that the antenna was effectively under water.

Was he going to have to clear all the snow off the roof? That would take a long time, and he would have to find a ladder.

He trudged in his snowshoes, circling around the house, looking for where the cable came through the wall.

It wasn't hard to find. There was a metal pipe clamped to the side of the house and right beside it, the cable appeared out of a hole surrounded by a black weather seal. It was folded into a loop right beside a hand-crank.

The radio antenna could be cranked to a higher position. Hurriedly, he gripped his gloved hands around the handle and tried to crank. It turned half a turn, before it came to a hard stop. Snow came tumbling down from the roof and landed on his head. He brushed it aside.

Something moved. That was a good sign. He worked at the crank again and a little bit of snow came down. But it wasn't enough. The antenna was still buried under the snow.

"Where did Gene hide his ladder?"

...

The ladder was in the garage, a separate building. Even finding the door required scraping away a snow drift. Luckily Gene hadn't stored his snow shovel in the garage, or it would have *really* taken a long time.

Once he'd opened the garage, he located Generator B. It was in pieces on the workbench, apparently being repaired when abandoned. The dust made him certain it wasn't the solar storm that chased Gene away—just normal life events.

Armed with the ladder and a broom, Will tackled the buried antenna.

A few feet up on the ladder, Will had a moment's panic when the legs settled and over he went, crashing into the snow.

First time I'm grateful for the snow. But I would have had a broken bone or at least bruises falling on the ground.

Up he went again, shaking the ladder side to side to wedge the legs deep into the snow to make his support more secure.

With the broom, he pushed the snow aside, conscious that if he bent any of the branches of the antenna, that he just might make it unusable. He worked gently.

Still the snow tumbled off, and the solar panels, two rows of them, came into view. He gave them an extra brush, trying to expose more of the surface to the light.

How much daylight is necessary to charge the batteries? And how come the batteries weren't already charged when he first tried them? He'd need to look at that again.

Once the antenna was exposed, he found a latch. Maybe that was what was keeping it from being cranked up to its full height.

Just then, sunlight broke through the clouds. It was blinding, reflecting off the white snow everywhere.

Please charge the batteries! My legs are killing me already.

Back on the ground, working the crank took some effort, but free of the clamp, the antenna went up and the loop of coax cable straightened out.

Panting from the exertion, he went back inside to warm up.

He treated himself to a late lunch and then skinned down to shorts. A quick check showed nothing coming in from the solar cells. But that was a problem for later.

He pedaled as hard as he could for ten minutes. He had to test the radio.

Randomly, he selected one of the contacts that had shown up in Gene's logbook. He set the dials. Faintly, there were voices and distant static—a good sign that the antenna was working.

He pressed the button.

"Hello, CQ for anyone in the Denver area. CQ CQ CQ. This is Breckenridge Colorado, looking for a contact in the Denver area. CQ CQ CQ."

He let up the button.

Behind some static came a woman's voice. "This is W5WEQ, in Aurora, calling Breckenridge."

"I hear you Aurora. It's so good to hear a voice! Breckenridge is buried in the snow. We're in the dark territory. No power. Over."

She chuckled, a grandmotherly voice. "You sound young. Over."

"Yes, high school, but I'm short on time. Battery will die quickly, I'm working off of a pedal-powered generator. Can I call you back in a little bit? Over."

"Yes, one hour from now? Over."

"That's fine. Is there power in your area? Over."

"Just recently. Power coming up all along Interstate 25. I heard about I-70 backed up with dead cars. Over."

"It's not just …. Inverter going." And the radios died.

Will shouted to the empty room. "It works! I made contact! It works."

He turned off the inverter and climbed back onto the bicycle.

As he cranked, he leaned over and picked up the blue radio.

"Will Parker calling Sheriff Thompson."

There wasn't a response.

"Kelly, are you there?"

"Yes, Will. What is it?"

"I made radio contact. Some lady in Aurora. They've got power in Denver. Over."

"That's great! Sheriff didn't answer? Over."

"He can't spend every minute glued to the radio. It can wait, but I'm glad you were there. I had to tell someone. Over."

"I've got a little news. Dad is somewhat better. I even took a quick little drive over to the mobile home park to let the Pattersons know what their father was up to. Over."

Will grinned as he pedaled. "Oh, I'm glad. Where they happy to hear the news?"

"Doug was a little worried when his father would get back. I had the chance to chat with Mary when he went to get some more rocks for their stove. Over."

"Oh, how did that go? Over."

"She loosened up a little once I confessed I had some guy troubles. I may have spun a little tale. Over."

"Don't get me in trouble! I have reason to suspect my folks think I've been fooling around. Over."

She chuckled. "Anyway Mary was very relieved to hear about … her father."

Thompson's voice broke in. "Sorry to interrupt, but is there news about the radio?"

Will quickly gave him the summary. "I'll have another contact in a few minutes once I've charged up the battery enough. My legs are really talking to me. Over."

Thompson gave him some questions to ask and promised to have a better list when he talked later.

Kelly turned him loose as well. He set aside the little phone and concentrated on the pedals.

...

"My name is Eve. Evelyn Madison, W5WEQ. What's your name, by the way, and your call sign? Over."

Will smiled. "I'm Will Parker, and I don't really have a call sign. I broke into this house to seek shelter when I was stranded in a snowstorm and only later discovered the radio equipment. The owner's call sign is W5KZZ. Over."

"That's Gene Barton's call sign. Oh, he's going to be ticked when he finds out that you broke in. Over."

"You know him? I guess you do at that. I called on this frequency because I found contact information in his logbook. All that I know about radio comes from his logbooks and the ARRL Handbook. But, it was necessary. Breckenridge really needs contact with Colorado's DHSEM or FEMA. The sheriff gave me phone numbers. Do you have phone service? Over."

"We have cell service. The land lines are still down. It's a shame, because I could have patched you through if the land line worked, but I can always hold my cell phone up to the radio here."

Will gave Eve the phone numbers and Thompson's name and who to ask for at the other end. They scheduled another contact at eight in the morning to confirm that she'd made it through the phone system, and then again at nine. He'd have Thompson on the blue phone at that time. It'd be a complicated mess, but if it worked Thompson would finally get to talk to people who might be able to help.

Eve asked, "Will, you know, your use of the radio, unlicensed like this is illegal. However, ham radio operators are really big on disaster relief. Sometimes, we're the only way people can get through, especially when the phone lines and the cell towers are all down.

"So, I'm not going to get all huffy about it. But, still, I'd like you to consider going ahead and getting your ham license once this is all done. If you can bring a home-brew rig like Gene's up cold with no outside help, then I think you've got the right stuff for it. Over."

Will chuckled. "Well, it is interesting, but I definitely don't have any money. It'll take a while before things get back to normal, no matter what. But, yeah. I might just do that."

Making Connections

Will made contact with Thompson and confirmed the morning call.

Then he rummaged through the pantry until he came up with oatmeal with honey for supper. He ate a healthy portion because he needed to pedal that bicycle for a couple of hours before he could afford to go to sleep.

"Will, are you there?"

"Yes, Kelly, I'm here, pedaling away."

She chuckled. "We're both going to have good legs before this is all over. Did you eat supper?"

He confessed that he had. She laughed at his taste in dishes.

"How about you?"

"I ate over at the school shelter. They're pretty organized, even if the portions are skimpy." She sighed. "I'll be sleeping in a chair tonight."

Will knew that he couldn't say anything too personal because, quite likely, someone at the sheriff's office was monitoring the radio.

"Close enough to hold his hand?" he asked.

"Probably not. That is a men's hospital room, after all. I'll probably sleep out in the hallway or maybe in the chapel. Hand-holding will have to wait for another time."

"There's something I need to warn you about. From eight until maybe ten in the morning, I'll be tied up on the ham radio. Nine to ten, or until the battery runs out, I'll be managing a conversation between Thompson and somebody in Denver who can help Breckenridge. So ... don't even try to call me on the blue radio during that time, okay?"

"That's great news! So your contact in Aurora is going to help."

"Yeah, she sounds like somebody's grandmother and she knows exactly who Gene Barton is. Supposedly Gene is off visiting family somewhere in Oklahoma. But ham radio people are big on helping during disasters, so we're in luck."

Kelly sounded relieved. "I'm so glad. Maybe the hospital can get the medicines they need."

"I have no idea what's first on the priority, but I guess that's not my job."

Kelly urged him to pedal hard, but to take breaks to charge up his fluids and carbs. He chuckled. She sounded like a coach.

· · ·

Sleeping alone, with no companionship other than the whistling of the wind outside, Will felt free to dream about Kelly. He held the spare pillow tight and imagined some time when all they had to worry about was sneaking away together.

Up before six, he traced the wires and found a circuit breaker on the solar panel wiring. He pushed it and crossed his fingers that would fix the problem. In any case, with fresh snow, he wasn't going to get any solar power juice today.

He pedaled the bike generator up until it was time to call Eve for their eight o'clock check in.

"Those bureaucrats made it hard to get through on the first call, but they gave me a special number to get straight through. We're supposed to talk to Harold Baker at nine. You have your guy cued up?"

"Yes, Sheriff Thompson. He's anxious to get this started."

She coached him on how to manage the call, and then they shut down to save his batteries until nine.

· · ·

Eve had a different tone in her voice, like she was a school teacher talking to boys.

"Gentlemen, we're ready to go, but I can't emphasize enough that you follow the procedure and say 'over' when you end talking. This conversation is going from a cell phone, through a little old lady with her ham radio, to a high school student who had to figure out his radio on his own, through a FRS radio to the Sheriff in Breckenridge. The high school student and the little old lady have to manage the push-to-talk buttons on all these radios and we can't know when you're done unless you say 'over'. Got that! Over."

The two men agreed, and then self-consciously added their overs.

Will said, "Sheriff Thompson, you go first. Over."

The radios all shifted their transmit and receive modes. Eve only had to manage her radio, but Will had to work both the ham radio button and the blue radio button as well. He hoped he didn't mess up too often.

The conversation quickly got technical. Thompson had an outline of what he needed to do to officially request assistance for Summit County and Breckenridge. He also had the names and requests of the police chief and the mayor.

"Summit County has been hit hard, and we really need an ongoing line of communication. What would it take to get the county's radio system linked back up with the state?"

There were other requests. One in particular had Will straining his ears to catch every word.

"St. Anthony Summit Medical Center has several patients that need to be transferred to hospitals with electricity and a more complete inventory of medicines. Some are in critical condition. Is it possible to arrange an airlift out? Road transport is flatly impossible. Over."

Baker asked, "What's the elevation there? Over."

"9160 feet at the hospital's helipad. Over."

"Hmm. How many people are we talking about? Over."

"I have a list."

Thompson gave the names and the doctor's recommendations. Sam Winslow was on the list—complications associated with pneumonia.

Baker asked for them to hold for a moment. It gave Will a chance to look at the little blue phone in his hand and notice that the minimal battery indicator showed two bars of four. From his experience, that meant the little FRS radio couldn't be counted on for any more long conversations. He'd have to come up with double-A batteries soon.

Baker came back on. "Can you be ready for an airlift in the morning? Say ten? Over."

"I'll arrange to have the helipad cleared. It's deep in snow at the moment, but I guarantee it'll be ready by then. Over."

There was some reporting, Thompson giving the DHSEM a run-down on their stocks of food and fuel. Thompson predicted that Hoosier Pass would be open within the week, unless they had another big snow move in.

Baker gave his assurances that the state and FEMA would make things better. "We've just been through this with Winter Park. They were isolated except for the train through Moffat Tunnel."

As the conversation stretched on, Will worried more about the little radio's batteries and he was personally grateful when Baker and Thompson agreed to schedule another radio meeting.

"Is that okay with you Mrs. Madison? Will?" Thompson asked.

"Oh, this is fine," she said. "I've had friends made snide remarks about my hobby for years and I'm just basking in the glow when I tell them how I'm saving Breckenridge. I can keep patching you through for as long as you need me."

"Well, I hope to get our official radios repaired. Will? Are you doing okay?"

"Yes. Fine." Surely he could find some double-A batteries before tomorrow. He hadn't checked nearly all the cabinets yet.

Thompson signed off and Eve asked, "Really, how are you holding up? I felt like you were a little slow with the buttons toward the last."

"Okay, really. I just started paying too much attention to the battery indicator on the FRS radio. It's showing half battery and I need to scare up some double-As before tomorrow."

"Well, if you don't find any, warn them ahead of time so you won't leave your sheriff cold if you drop out in the middle of the conversation."

Will promised he'd be ready. Eve signed off.

...

With the last cubbyhole checked, Will frowned at the little blue radio. It was all streamlined and user-friendly. But like all consumer electronics, it lived or died by its batteries.

No help for it.

He pressed the button to send the chime. Then he said, "This is Will, is Kelly Winslow there?"

After a long moment, Kelly answered, breathing hard. "Sorry. I left the radio on the cabinet. What's up?"

"Well, we had the first meeting."

"May I confess that Lucy and I—one of the nurses here—listened in? The place went into high gear when we heard that there was going to be a helicopter coming for some of the patients. There's a crew of volunteers scraping the snow off the parking lot, really the place with the big H where helicopters land."

"That's good. You know your father was on the list."

She sighed. "I know. But it's what I was praying for. He needs to be moved to a hospital that can fix him."

Will nodded to himself. And she needed to be there with him.

"I have a question about your radio. I'm at two bars on the battery indicator. How much talk time is that?"

"Hmm. It really depends. Do you have any replacement batteries?"

"No. I looked."

"Then, make sure you turn the radio all the way off until you expect a call. Even standby mode uses up some juice. Keep the volume low. And transmitting takes more power than receiving.

"And I guess I shouldn't chat with you like this. I'll check around to find replacement batteries for you, but for now, just save your juice."

"I know. And I'm sorry I can't talk. You go help your father. I'll get through this. Over and out."

He gave her a few seconds to reply, but when she didn't, he powered the radio all the way off. He hoped the sheriff office listened in so they would know the problem as well.

There's nothing I can do right now but go pedal the bicycle. We must have drained a lot of power this morning.

Saying Goodbye

Will startled awake when Kelly eased into bed beside him.

"Hey!"

She leaned closer. "Sorry to wake you up. You were really out of it. Pedal that bike too long?"

"Um." He tugged at the blanket. "Yeah, pretty wiped out. I didn't even hear the snowmobile. You did drive up, right?"

"Yes. I brought you some batteries."

"But what about your father? He's leaving in the morning. I half expected you to go with him."

By the light of the fire, he could see her sadness. "That was never in the cards. If I rode the helicopter, some needy patient would have to be bumped. They've promised me that when the road is cleared and there's a bus, they'll make sure I get to his new hospital, but I didn't like that idea either.

"Lucy, a nurse there, said she'd take care of me, but I had a talk with Daddy, once it was clear that he was being flown out. I've been taking care of myself even before this whole thing started. I don't need a parent substitute. I've got a home there at the lodge for at least a few more months. I've got people who care about me already keeping an eye on me.

"And more than that, I've got a job here. You maybe got the radio working, but I'm your caretaker and the one who has to bring you supplies."

She sighed. "Daddy didn't buy my argument totally, but he didn't really have any choice. He understood that I needed to get some batteries to you ASAP, so we had our tearful goodbyes and I headed this way."

"So ..." Will asked, "you are staying here for now?"

She smiled. "Any complaint?"

"Other than worries about your reputation, spending night after night alone with me."

She scooted closer, resting her arm across his chest. "I hate to tell you this, but as much as I insisted that nothing happened, nobody at the hospital, not my dad nor the nurse, nor even Mary Patterson believed me. Dad said he trusted me. But I could see it in his eyes that he had his doubts. Nurse Lucy smiled and said she believed me, but then not ten minutes later she had shifted the conversation around to birth control and what to do if a girl finds herself pregnant."

Will nodded. "I have very strong suspicions my parents are the same way." He sighed. "I don't even want to fight people about it. It's really nobody's business but ours."

Kelly sighed. "It sometimes feels like it's not worth the fight. I mean if nobody believes you anyway."

Will felt like he had this same conversation in a dream—a dream that got very intense. He wished it was that easy.

Instead, he said, "If nobody believes us, then that makes it all the more important that we stay true to ourselves. You made your rules so you could keep your self-respect. I'm committed to help you any way I can."

He shifted under the blanket. "So, I think maybe, that I need to wash up and get dressed for bed. I just collapsed here after cycling. And, um, I'm not really dressed properly."

She smiled. "You're not totally naked. I peeked."

Will shook his head. "We've got to work at this together. I *can't* make a move on you while you are emotionally vulnerable due to your father's illness. But that doesn't mean I'm made of stone either. Holding myself back takes a lot of effort, and I'm not sick and weak like I was before."

Kelly moved her hand and realized that below the blanket, there was indisputable evidence that what he was saying was true.

"Oh! I'm sorry. I thought . . . ."

"Kelly, we've got to stick to the rules we agreed to, especially when we're alone together. That said, I'll hold your hand and give you as many hugs as you need. Down the road, when we *really* know each other well, I'm all in favor of fun and games in bed and sage advice from Nurse Lucy. Okay?"

Kelly chuckled nervously. "Yeah, I was getting caught up in the moment. It's easy with you." She shifted position adding a little space between then. "And now that you mention it. You do smell a little ripe. Did you charge the battery all the way up?"

"Enough. And you brought double-A batteries?"

"Yep, a twelve-pack. That ought to last us."

"Then maybe I can get a good night's sleep. If you don't keep pestering me."

She chuckled. "I'll get some wash water for you."

She eased out of bed and took a bucket out the back door to get some fresh snow. The instant she was out of sight, he made a dash for the bathroom.

I really do need a cold shower, but any bath will help.

. . .

It felt like he'd been cooped up in the house forever. With the morning sun beaming down on him, sitting down on snowmobile and gripping the handles felt really good. Kelly climbed on behind him.

"They're supposed to arrive at ten? Do we have time?"

Will shrugged. "I don't know. It depends on what route the helicopter takes. Surely they have to go through one of the passes to get here."

They roared down the road, looking for anyplace that might have a view down into the valley.

The cold wind was refreshing at first, but numbing on his face after a bit. Kelly's grip around his waist felt good, but he knew she was worried about her father.

"There!" she pointed. From their elevation, he could see down into the valley, mostly a white blanket, with the deep channel that was the snow-plowed highway. He pulled to a stop.

As soon as the engine noise died, he could hear it. The helicopter was barely large enough to see, but its rhythmic sound echoed up the valley.

"It's getting lower." But quickly it was out of sight, around the bend, landing at the hospital. "Do you want to wait here?"

"If we could." She was quiet. Clearly they had no chance of getting to the hospital in time. She had gotten the urge to see him off a little too late in the morning.

"Come up here." He took her hand and helped her sit sideways in his lap. He put his arms around her, just doing what he could to make her feel better.

"It feels like he'll never come back."

He shook his head. "That's not logical. With better medical care he'll get well, and then his first priority will be to come back here to get his daughter—not to mention all his fancy ski gear."

She laughed, almost sincerely. "You're right there. All his stuff is at the lodge. His skis and other gear, not to mention his Olympic medal."

Will asked, "What do you have that you can't live without?"

It was an idle question, just designed to keep her mind off what was happening down at the hospital. She seemed to take it seriously.

"All my clothes. I've been living in these things for far too long. If I had something to change into, I'd burn these."

"Hey there. Wait until the shops open back up before burning anything."

"You think the shops will open?"

"Oh, sure. When they get the diesel, they can run the snow plows. Once the gas stations open up, cars will come and go. Even if they can't take credit cards with the fancy machines, the shop owners will write down the numbers and make those sales."

"You think people will come?"

"Tourists? Of course. A disaster is just another tourist draw. And people here will welcome them. Once the gold mines dried up, it's been tourism that keeps people coming to Breckenridge. It's the primary economy."

"But when? It still feels to me that we're still caught in a trap. No power, no internet. No way in or out."

Will held up his glove to catch the sunlight. "Oh, I feel the thaw. We started it. You and me. We'll go back to the cabin and manage another conversation between Breckenridge and the outside world in just a little bit. We've already got our first delivery of help, down in that helicopter. We'll get more, just as soon as Rick and Nick and all the others cut through the Blue River avalanche and open the road.

"More help will arrive, and as soon as the gas stations can pump gas, the stranded tourists will leave to go fix up their lives.

"My job will be to help get the lodge back in shape for the arrival of the new tourists, and the cycle will start up all over again."

"Even without power and heat?"

"That will come. See, you can just make out the solar farm down there. Maybe we'll only get electricity for a few hours in the middle of the day, but it'll be enough to find everything that burned out and repair them. Eventually, the big power lines will hum again.

"Until then, I suspect the lodge will heat rocks for the rooms, just like the mobile home park people do. For a short time at least, living with a rustic edge will be a tourist draw."

Kelly leaned closer into his arms. "At least you can see a future. I'm not so sure of mine. I'm one of those tourists who has to leave to go fix up a broken life."

"We'll see about that. Just consider that we're going to be together today, tomorrow, and for weeks or months. We've got plenty of time to figure out how to keep that going."

Not too long after that, they heard the beat of the helicopter's blades. They watched as the military craft followed the Blue River up the valley, and then returned just a few minutes later.

"They needed to get an overview of the town, I guess."

And then the helicopter vanished behind Swan Mountain, finding its route back to Denver.

Kelly sighed. "He's really gone."

Will held her tight.

Packing Up

The helicopter's appearance sparked a surge of optimism in Breckenridge. Before, it had been all to easy to think that the whole world had collapsed into darkness, with no improvement in sight.

Now, it was clear that they were being rescued, and there was a normal life just over the mountains.

Thompson was almost bubbly as he checked in with them.

"Yes, the hospital got most of the goodies, but we've got a radio repairman with a big kit of spares. He seems to think that we can get Summit County's Comm Center up and running, and with a connection to a repeater up Loveland Pass, we can have direct communication to the outside world."

Will said, "That's great. Not that I don't mind being right in the middle of all this important stuff, but I worry about how patient Eve Madison will be. How long does your repairman predict this will take?"

Thompson hesitated. "If it was just you, I wouldn't mind keeping you on call for another week, not that your parents are happy with this. You don't mind, do you?"

"No, we're fine. The pantry is getting a little thin, but we can make it and we have the snowmobile to resupply if necessary."

"Hmm. The repairman has a satellite phone, but unfortunately, so many of the satellites were damaged by the CME, he says, that it's hit or miss getting through that way. So I really need you there to make the calls. My best guess is three to four days. Then you can come home. Is that okay?"

"That will work. And when you see my folks, tell them I'm behaving myself—not that they'll believe it."

"Hey," he chuckled, "that's not my job, but call me if you have any *other* problems."

...

It was a day later, just after sunset with lit candles so they could walk around, when Kelly hurried into the radio room.

Will paused his cycling. "What's the matter? You look like you saw a ghost."

She leaned up against the wall, away from the door. She whispered, "The guy with the gun. I saw him sneaking up along the edge of the road, coming this way."

Will frowned. "A neighborly visit?"

She didn't look convinced.

Will considered the issues. The guy had been holed up in his place since the power went down. How were his supplies holding out?

The two of them hadn't been keeping a very low profile, coming and going on the snowmobile. Did he know for sure that they weren't neighbors? Was he still convinced they were looters?

In any case, he didn't want to face a man with a gun, but what could they do?

"Kelly? Do you have your radio?"

She pointed to the handset resting on the table next to the ham set.

"No, the other one." She had brought her father's radio with her, since it would be useless and likely lost if he took it with him to Denver.

She whispered, "In my jacket pocket."

"Come over here." He took the FRS radio on the table and turned it to receive, then he switched the house speakers on. He pointed to the ham radio's microphone and tapped the push-to-talk button. The transmitter wasn't on, but that wasn't what he was trying to do. "Hold this down."

She nodded.

He slipped out of the radio room into the dark storeroom. He got down on the floor and crawled over to where Kelly's jacket was draped. He fished out the identical little blue radio and pressed the transmit button.

"This is Will Parker calling Sheriff Thompson. Are you there?" His words echoed out the front porch speakers.

He moved carefully across the floor until he could peer out the window.

The man holding the gun had frozen in position at the words.

"This is Thompson. Hello, Will. Do you have a problem?" His words were also being picked up by the handset in the radio room.

"Um. I just wanted you to know that we've noticed that man with the gun. You know the one we mentioned several days ago? Well, he's been lurking around the house and I thought you should know."

"Stay indoors and out of sight. I can get a snowcat up there, but not quickly."

"Well, Sheriff, he hasn't made any aggressive moves. No threats or gunshots. Not like last time. If he could hear your voice right now, what would you want to say to him."

"Like on a speaker?"

"Exactly like that."

"Well. Hmm. I'd say that there was no need for a man to pull out a gun, especially not now that things were turning around. We actually broke through the Blue River avalanche and the road should be clear by morning. There's a tanker truck of diesel waiting just on the other side of Hoosier Pass earmarked for us.

"With that diesel, and with a couple of loaner snowplows from Park County, we'll start clearing the roads almost immediately. It won't be all that long before the people out on Snow Hill Road will start seeing some activity coming their direction.

"And by the way. We've got two more food trucks heading for Breckenridge.

"Anyone who has been hunkered down and waiting out the snow should start to see relief sooner than they expected. All it takes is a little more patience. Now is not the time to make desperation moves with a gun."

Will saw the man turn around and head back the way he came.

...

And then, it was the day to pack up.

Kelly asked, "Are you sure you want to detail *all* the stuff we did here?"

Will was in the fourth sheet writing down all the changes he made to the radio, all the food they raided out of the pantry, the wood they burned, and of course, the window he broke.

"I'm not mentioning that I slept several nights on the sleeper-sofa with my girlfriend dressed in Mrs. Barton's nightgown. Were you worried about that?"

She sniffed and went to tighten the straps on the snowmobile again. It was going to be very tight getting all their stuff down the mountain.

Will turned back to the paper.

And one final note, Mr. Barton, I want you to know how important your ham radio and your off-grid power proved to be to Breckenridge. Before I had to seek shelter in your place during the worst of the snows, things were looking pretty bleak here, but with the help of your radio and with the help of Eve Madison W5WEQ in Aurora, Breckenridge was able to call for the help it needed. I am personally very grateful.

...

Will squeezed into place on the snowmobile.

Kelly took a long look at the house where they'd stayed. "I don't really want to leave," she said.

He smiled. "I know what you mean. It was a nice place."

"More than that," she smiled. "It was a place where we didn't have to ask permission to be together."

He nodded. "I won't be asking permission anymore."

"Oh? What will your parents say about that?"

"I hope they'll say, 'He's grown up.' But it doesn't matter."

She nodded thoughtfully. "You're right. It's up to us now. You know, I'm going to have to rethink some things."

"Like what?"

"Like the way I judged Beth and my mother. I can't really frown at them for needing a man in their lives. Not anymore."

Will understood. "Take your time and be true to yourself. I'll be right there with you."

She grinned and shook her ski poles. "Race you back?"
He sighed. "I'll never beat you."
"I know."

Epilogue

One week before Christmas, City Market opened for business and Breckenridge celebrated the season with so many candle-lit dinners that in subsequent years, it became a tradition.

Sam Winslow made it back to Breckenridge just in time to sit at the Parker family table. He watched with interest as his daughter worked so closely with May Parker as they prepared the food and laid out the table.

Beth had taken the bus back to Denver, alone. Kyle had left to return to Kansas a few days earlier. Jess Baxter had recovered his car from the parking garage with so little fanfare than Will hadn't noticed until he was gone.

Bob Parker asked, "Are you going to resume your training for the Olympics?"

Sam shook his head. "After so many days flat on my back in the hospital, I doubt I'll be able to get back into shape. In fact, I've been thinking about something Kelly mentioned a while back. I think I'll open a ski school here in Breckenridge. So many places have gone out of business that this might just be the ideal time to snap up one of the storefronts and hang out a sign. I bet Kelly could teach a few classes, too."

Will and Kelly exchanged glances. It had taken a lot of selling on Kelly's part to make the case that her father should become an instructor, but she was sure he would be good at it.

And Kelly would be in Breckenridge for the long term.

Will went back to high school once classes started up again. The year had an abbreviated schedule, but it would be enough to get him his diploma and move on to Colorado Mountain College in the fall.

He shared a bit of school gossip with Kelly. Rick and Mary were openly going together. There was some speculation about them, but Will disclaimed all interest. He didn't care to have people asking personal questions about Kelly and preferred to give Rick and Mary the same deference.

The Torinos had moved into one of the FEMA trailers that had arrived once the Eisenhower Tunnel was reopened. Interstate 70 was hardly cleared of all of the abandoned vehicles, many of which were still buried in the snow, but there was through traffic in both directions.

Hefty generators were purchased and even though the city had limited electricity, the gondola and many of the ski lifts were open for business. Tourism was the lifeblood of Breckenridge and nationwide advertising started claiming that with the deep snow, ski season would likely last through August. At night, the generators added their power to the local electric grid.

By February, cell phone coverage was restored, with newly-installed microwave links over the mountains. There was a huge cheer of relief from the merchants as they were finally able to run the credit cards with ease again. Land lines were still out, but for many, that made little difference.

But the big power lines were still down. One of the major feeds into the area had towers knocked down by the Swan Mountain avalanche and the whole area was so deep in snow that repair crews couldn't get their vehicles and cranes into place to make the repairs.

By summer, when the snow stopped falling, Breckenridge felt back to normal, with the look of fresh construction all around. When the River Mountain Lodge had their annual owners meeting, in spite of some absentee owners angry at the repair work needed on their units, Bob Parker was retained as manager and commended for the work he had done to take care of the guests during the catastrophe.

. . .

Kelly asked, "What are you doing?"

Will leaned back from the computer. "Just checking the calendar. Too much to do."

She sat down in his lap. "Show me."

He held her waist with one hand and moved the other across the trackpad. He sighed. "I'm taking business classes at the college to make my parents happy, getting a network certificate, because I could use an entry into the job market, and studying on my own to get my ham license.

"You need to start paying attention to this stuff too. If you wanted to relocate to Steamboat Springs, they have a ski and snowboard business degree."

"Only if you wanted to come with me. But honestly, I couldn't leave Dad alone to run the business. I probably know most of what they teach anyway."

"Maybe," he said. "Some of these business classes are opening my eyes a bit. My father was doing a lot more than I realized."

She pointed at a day marked with a star. "What's this?"

He chuckled. "Our one year anniversary. Don't you remember? It's coming up fast."

She leaned back against him. "I haven't forgotten. That's the day we get more serious, isn't it?"

"That's what I was told, by someone who had her rules."

She put her arm around his neck. "Just how serious do you want to get?"

"All the way serious, public and private."

They sagged into a deep kiss. She whispered. "That's the answer I was hoping for."

END

References

The Big Snow of 1898-9

While you can find articles on the Big Snow on the Internet, nearly all of them referenced the book **Summit** by Mary Ellen Gilliland. I picked up a used copy on Amazon and it was well worth it. This is a massive tome of information and if you have any interest in the history of Summit County, then it's your first choice.

The Solar Storm of 1859

Wikipedia is a great starting point. The article is interesting, but the References section that follows it leads you down the rabbit hole to more articles about solar storms and related history than you can imagine. If you're fearful of what the future might bring, you might just want to pretend this is just fiction and leave it at that.

As a science fair project, tracking sunspots to calculate the rotation of the sun worked out pretty well for my daughter. Just make sure you get a scope with a proper sun filter and a way to take pictures, lots of pictures. Who knows what you might see.

https:/en.wikipedia.org/wiki/Solar_storm_of_1859

Amateur Radio

I grew up in a house with a radio room much like the one depicted in this book. My parents Gene Melton (W5KZZ) and Evelyn Melton (W5WEQ) were hams, as was my elder brother. I was the black sheep of the family, unable to learn Morse Code, which was a necessity to get a ham license back then. However, I absorbed enough of the technical information to get a commercial radio license when I went off to college, letting me earn a living working for radio and TV stations in Austin, Texas.

The ARRL Handbook has many editions, so it's easy to find. There are also study guides to walk you through the tests. If you've ever wanted to push the limits of what you can do with radio, or wanted to be the person who can help in emergencies, this is a hobby that can change lives.

If you want more books like this, consider leaving a review on your favorite online bookstore or review service.

Other books by Henry Melton include a number of young adult adventures, mainly science fiction. A few recommendations to start with are:
Emperor Dad
Extreme Makeover
Falling Bakward
Golden Girl
and many others.

In addition, there is the Project Saga, a multi-generation future epic spanning centuries.
Begin with: Star Time